Welcome to the
The Accidental Mystery Series.

Books in the series:

And So To Sleep
And So To Dream
The Wrath of Grapes
And So To Love
And So It Goes

Hi Betty
Read on!
Emily Allen Harper

AND SO

IT

GOES

EVELYN ALLEN HARPER

CHAPTER 1

IT WAS THE first summer in her memory that she hadn't found a four-leaf clover. It wasn't as if she had actively looked for them. Well, sometimes she did, but it often appeared as if they were looking for her. A casual stroll across the lawn, a glance down at the ground and, in the middle of a patch of three-leaved clovers, one would jump out at her. As a child, she'd stop in the middle of running when a four-leaf clover seemed to pop up, just for her.

If she hadn't thought about it, not finding one wouldn't have bothered her. But once she had, it became an obsession. Did not finding one mean something? Good luck had followed her all her life, but then she had been finding four-leaf clovers all those summers.

Fearful that there was a deeper, darker meaning in her failed quest, she found herself inventing excuses to walk in unexplored areas, going further and further away from the house, her eyes not on the beautiful countryside, but on the grassy areas beside the road.

And there, with its head poking higher than any of the weeds and clover surrounding it, was the biggest, most beautiful four-leaf clover that she had ever seen.

Letting out a big sigh, she was surprised that finding the clover was such a relief. If you'd have asked her before this four-leaf cloverless summer, she would have assured you that she didn't have a superstitious bone in her body.

With her arms outstretched, she worked her way into the ditch, separating the weeds as she went. Within reach of the clover, her foot caught on something. Concentrating on picking her prize while maintaining her balance, she waited until the clover was safely in her possession before she glanced down to see what had caused her to stumble.

Half concealed by the weeds lay a man dressed in formal attire. Stifling a scream, she staggered out of the ditch. Too shocked to think clearly, she stood on quivering legs in the middle of the logging road, still clutching her good-luck clover in a shaky hand.

The scene, the makings of a very bad dream, quickly turned into a nightmare when the man raised his head and looked at her. Stunned, her mouth went dry and her heart lurched; shaking her head, she backed away. When his mouth began to move and his pleading eyes begged her to listen, she fought the urge to flee, but could she really run away from someone who so desperately needed help?

Stepping closer, her eyes found the source of the heavy flow of blood that was forming a puddle in the ditch; the man had been shot in the chest. Now, realizing that he was in no condition to harm her, she pushed aside the weeds to kneel by his side, her ear close to his mouth.

In the bushes across the two-track road, another man, also dressed in formal attire, was seething at the intrusion. In his rush to hide from the unexpected nosy walker, his only choice had been a slender tree. Trying to make himself fit behind it, he was standing sideways, watching. Where had she come from? The last thing he needed was a witness.

He held his breath as he watched her put her head down, looking as if she were listening. Reality hit when the woman removed a cell phone from her pocket while raising her eyes to scan the area.

Damn! His well-aimed first bullet hadn't finished the job! The woman probably had been told his name and she was about to share it.

Stepping out from behind the tree, he took aim and fired.

The woman, with a phone in one hand and the prized four-leaf clover in the other, gasped. With wild eyes looking directly at her killer, she tumbled backward, landing on the man in the ditch. Since she wasn't alive when a second bullet whizzed past her, she never felt the body under her give one last shudder.

CHAPTER 2

THE OFFICE OF Allen Real Estate was ringing with the sound of happy babies and a cooing admirer. Molly Allen Hatch, owner of the agency, had dropped in to visit with Clara, the agent on duty. The twins, Tom and Jill, were crawling over the office floor, picking up bits and pieces of God-knows-what and putting them into their mouths.

Molly threw her hands up in surrender. "When I think of all those months that I sterilized everything that went into their mouths…!"

Clara laughed. "A little dirt never hurt anyone! Probably builds up their immune system."

"How's married life treating you?" Molly asked Clara, whose wedding ring was so new it practically had the price tag still attached to it.

"Well, it certainly has taken a lot of adjustment! I went from being the sole occupant of a house to being the mother of three small boys, plus having a new husband. I'm learning the art of multitasking."

"And what about Jerry? Are Joe's two boys accepting him?"

"Seems like it. There was a bit of jealousy at first, but that was to be expected. As you know, Joe fell in love with Jerry after he rescued him from the burning building, and for a while he was so obsessed with finding the boy's family, he neglected me and his own two boys. I know I was jealous."

No one spoke for a moment. Both women were remembering the problems Clara's jealousy had caused. It had almost broken the relationship between Joe and Clara prior to their marriage.

8

Trying to change the subject, Clara said, "I was surprised to see that it was you pushing the stroller. Nurse Anita is usually the one who brings the twins in to see me."

"I gave Anita the morning off. The last I saw her, she was heading out for a walk. Lately, she has been taking longer walks. I *do* hope nothing is bothering her, because I need her. I don't know if I could handle the twins, plus Mitch's two nieces, without her help."

Molly was busy prying a foreign object out of Tom's mouth when the door opened and two men walked in. The tall one, who seemed to be in charge, looked over the domestic scene of women and babies. "This *is* a real estate office, isn't it?"

Clara stood up from behind the desk. "Good morning," she called cheerily. "This is truly a real estate office. I'm Clara Skinner, the agent on duty right now. The woman with the babies is Molly Hatch, the owner of Allen Real Estate. She just dropped in to let me play with her twins for a bit."

Scooping up the twins, Molly secured them in the double stroller. "I'll get out of your way, Clara," she exclaimed as she headed past the men on her way to the door.

"Cute kids," the shorter of the two men commented as they walked past them.

"You're in good hands," Molly remarked to the two men. "Clara will take good care of you. She's the best agent in town!"

The door closed behind them.

Clara studied the shorter and younger man who had made the comment. He was watching Molly's departure with interest. Clara wondered if his attention was on redheaded green-eyed Molly or the twins.

"How may I hel…"

The door flew open, and a wild-eyed Detective Mitch Hatch stormed into the office. "Where's Molly?"

"She just left! You probably can catch her because she has the twins in the stroller. What in the world is going on, Mitch?"

"Anita's been murdered!" he yelled as he turned around and raced out the door.

CHAPTER 3

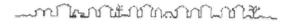

POLICE CARS AND ambulances lined the old logging road. Yellow tape sectioned off a large rectangular area that included the ditch where the two bodies lay, then stretched across the dirt road to seal off the area around a small tree.

Officer Tom Allen, who had just arrived on the scene, approached his sister's husband, Detective Mitch Hatch. The detective was standing by the ditch surveying the carnage.

Mitch turned his head and nodded to Tom. "This is a sight I never imagined seeing! That's Anita, Tom. She cooked my breakfast this morning." He paused to silence a sob. "What in the hell is she doing in the ditch with that man?"

"Any idea who he is?"

"Not yet. We're waiting for the rest of the crew to get here. I'm not the lead detective in this case. Captain Hilburn says I'm too close to one of the subjects."

"What do you make of this?"

"Molly is going to take this really hard. Anita has been with us since before the twins were born."

"That's not what I meant."

"I know what you meant, Tom, but I just can't make myself believe that Anita had anything to do with the man in the ditch."

"How sure of that are you? How well did you really know Anita?"

"How well do we ever know anyone? All I can say is that in the year that she's lived with us, she's never mentioned a man, or a family member, either. According to her, she was an only child and her parents are dead."

"Well, she died in the arms of that man. Think it might have been a jealous wife that pulled the trigger?"

"Not unless the wife was wearing a dark suit. They've found some material that got caught on the branch of the tree," Mitch said as he pointed. "The killer stood over there and shot them both; they've found the casings. But the first time the man was shot was at close range…there are powder burns on his clothes."

"So he was shot twice?"

"Looks like it. We'll have to wait for the autopsy to get the full story."

"Could it be that Anita just stumbled into a bad situation?" Tom wondered.

Mitch sighed. "Anita had such a big heart. If she saw someone in trouble, she'd have tried to help. She is, eh, was, a nurse, you know."

"Maybe he was still alive. If the killer was in the area, he couldn't take the chance that the victim hadn't told Anita who had shot him."

Both men grew quiet, watching the activities going on around them. Cameras flashed as the lead detective and the coroner did their jobs.

"I see that they are putting Detective Miller on the case."

"Yes, but that's not going to stop me from working on it. I feel that I owe Anita that much."

"This is quite a hike from your house. Any idea why she was walking so far out here in the woods?"

"Molly did say that Anita had taken up walking long distances lately. She never told Molly why, and Molly didn't want to pry. She was just hoping that Anita wasn't having some kind of problem that would interfere with her staying with us."

They stopped talking while they watched both bodies being placed on stretchers and carried off to separate ambulances.

Sirens aren't needed when the destination is the morgue.

CHAPTER 4

EMILY MILLS FULLER preened in front of the three-way mirror. Mike was right. The soft rose-colored business suit said several things about her. It made her look approachable while allowing her to appear aloof and untouchable. Sometimes at these book signings, the appreciative readers became aggressive while trying to gain her attention.

After her author-sister's murder, Emily had finished the book that Debra had left in her computer. Since Emily had never before given a thought to becoming a writer, it surprised her that she was quite good at it. In fact, the critics suggested that, of the two sisters, she was the one with the writing talent.

She had started a series of her own. Hot off the press, today was the big formal introduction of the first book in that series. Mike had arranged a large catered affair at the town's country club.

Emily had married her physical therapist shortly after the sordid publicity surrounding her then husband, Senator Jerome Mills, died down. Jerome had run an unsuccessful bid to head the presidential ticket in the up-coming national election. He was already out of the running when a packet of damning details had been mailed to the chairman of the opposition party. Emily, who had no idea what was in the packet, had mailed it, thinking it was something Jerome had just forgotten to do. The packet that had been put together over the years by Emily's writer-sister, Debra, contained details of Jerome's affairs, including the one with Ann, who had borne Jerome's son. Since both

Debra and Ann's lives had ended violently, Jerome was the prime suspect. He had gotten out of paying for his crimes by clutching his chest and dying when Emily informed him that she had mailed the envelope.

Looking at the diamond-encrusted watch on her arm, she frowned. Where was Mike? Whoever heard of an author being late for her own book signing? Since he had made all the plans, she was surprised that he wasn't here with her, looking incredibly handsome in his tuxedo.

She smiled when another memory of Mike in a tuxedo took her back to their wedding day. All the detail had been taken care of, and everyone was seated, but the minister had been late in arriving at the house. Their relief of having the minister finally show up was short-lived because, when he'd walked into the room, he brought with him the odor of something really dead. She had gagged. How was she supposed to get through the ceremony if she couldn't take a deep breath? She had looked at Mike for reassurance that he'd do what was necessary to correct the problem; he had rolled his eyes and shrugged. How do you tell a man of the cloth, a reverend, a man anointed by God, that he smelled? And not only did he stink, he was acting very peculiar.

Alarmed, she and Mike had looked sideways at each other. The minister, who had come with such high recommendations, was waving his hands in the air, ranting about smelly dog treats and idiot people who include animals in their marriage ceremony and could someone please direct him to the laundry room and a bottle of bleach? Together they had watched as the minister opened the bottle and poured bleach over his hands. His story of how a dog had been trained to be a member of the wedding party by using a smelly treat as an incentive had them laughing through most of the ceremony. The laughter that had started at the beginning of their union had continued through the days and weeks that followed.

Sometimes, when comparing her two marriages, Emily actually pinched herself. In her memory, the years she had spent with Jerome were colorless. Life with Mike, however, was filled with everything that had been missing in her first marriage. Living with someone she loved was a new experience that she reveled in every day she woke up in bed with Mike beside her.

Where was he? He certainly knew how important this event was to her. He had planned it, for heaven's sake! The later it got, the more she fumed. For the first time in her short marriage to Mike, she was thinking unkind thoughts. Words were building up inside her, words that she planned to pour over his head once he walked through the door. How dare he spoil her special day!

The ringing of the doorbell was a relief of sorts. Had Mike gone out and not taken his house key with him? With an impatient huff, she threw open the door. Standing in front of her were two uniformed officers. They didn't have to say a word. Knowing by the look on their faces, whatever they had to tell her, her life was never going to be the same again; she wilted.

———————

EMILY FOUND REFUGE in her locked bedroom. Hugging Mike's pillow and inhaling his smell was her only hold on sanity. None of it made sense. The police had so many questions for which Emily had no answers. She knew nothing about Mike's business, his clients, his co-workers, his family, or even his friends.

Her affair with him had started while she was still married to Senator Jerome Mills. Since they had to operate under the radar of the press, the affair was clandestine. She didn't have the chance to associate with anyone connected to the man with whom she had fallen in love. The two of them had their own little world.

After the death of Jerome and the need for secrecy was gone, the affair had come out of the shadows. Their circle of friends should have grown, but that had never happened. The two of them were content with each other. She knew that now she should be contacting someone to tell them that Mike was dead, but without an address book, a journal, or some other list to tell her who these people were, she was at a loss. Did he have living parents, siblings, maybe an ex-wife? How could she have been married to someone that she knew nothing about? Love may be blind, but this went way beyond blindness.

Mike's pillow was damp with her tears. Who hated Mike? The realization that Mike was gone forever ran in an unending loop in her head. She felt it as a physical blow when the reality of her loss hit her again. The man whom she'd loved had died all alone in a ditch. The terrifying realization of how scared he must have been as he faced his executioner brought a new burst of tears. What were his last thoughts? Did he think of her? No one was left from her family, and Mike seemed to have sprung from nothing.

CHAPTER 5

FOR THE FIRST time in its history, in the middle of the day there was a big CLOSED sign on the window of Allen Real Estate.

Upon hearing Mitch shout the news that Anita had been murdered, Clara snatched her purse, slapped the sign on the window, and locked the door. Now was not a time to sell a house; now was the time to find Molly and help her. Anita had become so much more than just live-in...she had become a friend.

Standing outside the office, she looked up and down the sidewalk. Where had Molly gone, and had Mitch found her? About to walk away, she stopped in her tracks. A faint whine coming from within the office was rapidly turning into a howl. Clara slapped her hand on her forehead. Lucky. She had forgotten the huge black dog that had been sound asleep in the corner.

Unlocking and opening the door, she was met with accusing brown eyes. "Sorry, old man! I sure did forget about you!"

Now, she had a problem. Since Lucky wouldn't ride in or on anything but a fire truck, she was stuck. Joe, Clara's new husband, was the captain of the fire station that was just around the corner.

"Let's go see Joe!" she said to the dog. Lucky's ears went up, his tail wagged, and with a doggy smile, he headed in that direction.

Joe was pulling into the station when he saw Clara and Lucky heading his way. Opening the van's door, he helped three boys unbuckle their safety belts, and then watched them as they raced down the sidewalk in Lucky's direction. Since their recent marriage and the adoption of Jerry, Clara and Joe had been sharing the load of taking care of him and Joe's two boys from his first marriage. Complicating the complexity of whose turn it was to be in charge for any given day, was Lucky. Because of his refusal to ride in a car, Clara had walked with him to work this morning, and someone was going to have to walk him home at the end of the day. Leaving him at home was not an option. He howled.

"Shouldn't you be at the office?" Joe called to Clara as she came into range.

Clara stopped walking and waited for Joe to come to her. "I have something to tell you, but I don't think little ears should hear what I have to say."

One look at his wife's face was enough to convince him. "Hey men!" he yelled to the boys. "Go and see if Dave has any more of those smelly treats for Lucky. Maybe he'll even teach the dog a new trick!"

The boys and the dog ran off in search of Dave. Ten-year-old Mackie, fair-haired like Joe's first wife, led the pack. Close on his heels was his younger dark-haired brother, Billy, a replica of his dad. Bringing up the rear was towheaded Jerry. When authorities were unable to discover the identity of the boy, Joe and Clara had adopted him. Lucky, his mouth watering at the mention of the treat, ran after them.

Turning to his wife, Joe raised his eyebrows. "So?" he said. "What is it that the boys shouldn't hear?"

"Anita has been murdered."

"What?"

"Anita has been murdered."

"I heard you the first time! But it doesn't make any sense. Who would want to harm such a nice person?"

"Mitch stuck his head into the office looking for Molly. She and the twins had just left, so she couldn't have gone too far. He just yelled that

Anita had been murdered, and then he took off. Now, you know as much as I do."

They stood in silence for a moment.

"Did you close the office?"

Clara nodded. "I need to go to Molly."

Without saying a word, Joe handed her the van's keys. "Go do what you can. I'll keep the boys and the dog with me, but you'll have to come back with the van. The boys will need a ride home, and then someone..." and here Joe rolled his eyes, "someone is going to have to walk Lucky home."

Clara grew pensive. "Joe, you know how much I love that dog." She paused, thinking about how Lucky had changed her life and all the special things he had done. "But," she stopped to take a big breath, "is he going to be the last straw that'll make our new family arrangements impossible?"

"What are you talking about? Sounds like you want to get rid of Lucky!"

"You know I don't want to get rid of him! But think about it, Joe. Walking him back and forth every day is just one more thing on top of all the other adjustments we've had to make. If only he'd get into a car! But he won't, and it would take a crane to pick him up and put him in one. I can't see that happening."

Joe shook his head. "Lucky saved my life when he threw his body over me when the fire truck exploded. We are *not* getting rid of him; I owe him that much. Anyhow, getting him into a car would just make another problem."

"Another problem? How so?"

"Clara, have you forgotten just how huge Lucky is? If we did ever get him into the car, there would be no room for anyone else!"

Clara threw her arms around Joe. "You are so good for me," she whispered as she kissed his neck. "You make me see the funny side of

20

things. But what I have to do now is not going to be fun." She held up the keys. "Gotta go. I'll keep you informed, and I'll be back with the van to take the boys home."

With a smile, she added, "Guess that means you're the one to walk Lucky home today."

Clara pulled the van into Molly's driveway. Seeing both cars in the open garage assured her that Mitch had found his wife.

She rang the bell.

Nothing happened. She put her ear close to the door, hoping to hear sounds of movement.

She rang the bell again.

Finally, she heard footsteps approaching the door, but the door didn't open.

"Hello?" Clara called.

"Who's there?" the tentative voice of a child asked.

"Clara. And who are you?"

"I'm Laurie."

"May I come in?"

"I don't think so."

"Could I talk to your Uncle Mitch?"

"I don't think so."

"You *do* know who I am, don't you, Laurie? I work with your Aunt Molly."

"I know who you are."

"So why can't I come in?"

"Because something bad is going on. Uncle Mitch and Aunt Molly are locked in their bedroom. I can hear Aunt Molly crying."

"Didn't they tell you anything before they locked themselves in? And by the way, is Kim with you?"

21

"No, they didn't tell us anything, and Kim is so scared, she's hiding in our closet."

"Then you'd better let me in. They would want you to do this."

"How do you know that? I don't want to get into trouble."

"I promise you, you won't get into trouble. Now open the door, please."

The door slowly opened. When Clara saw the scared eleven-year-old Laurie, her eyes red from crying, she opened her arms; the young girl threw herself into them.

"There, there," Clara murmured as she comforted Laurie. "Let's go get Kim out of the closet, and then we can talk."

"Where's Anita?" sobbed Laurie. "Uncle Mitch won't tell us anything! Why didn't she come back from her walk?"

Clara cringed. It wasn't her job to tell Mitch's nieces that their live-in nurse was never coming back from her walk.

"We'll talk about it," she promised. "Now take me to Kim."

Laurie took Clara's hand and led her up the stairs and down the hall past the master bedroom. The sounds coming out of that bedroom were not good. Clara squeezed Laurie's hand to keep her from stopping by the door.

"Let's let them be alone for a bit longer. Okay?"

Laurie nodded.

Kim, indeed, was hiding in the closet. It was a deep closet, and Kim had managed to squeeze herself into the furthest corner.

"You can come out now!" Laurie called to her sister. "Clara's here."

"Are we in trouble?" Kim whispered voice came from the closet's recess.

"No, Kim, you aren't in trouble," Clara answered. "Something has happened that has upset Molly and Mitch. It's not about either of you, so come on out and join us."

There was a moment of silence, and then eight-year-old Kim scooted out of the closet, bringing dust bunnies along with her. When Kim screwed up her face and exploded with a big sneeze, both girls giggled. For the first time since she had arrived, Clara felt as if she could handle the situation.

When Mitch's brother and his wife had been killed in an auto accident, Mitch had taken in their two young daughters, Laurie and Kim. His parents, now in their late seventies, were relieved to have him handle the responsibility of raising the girls. He had been a bachelor with two dependents when he met Molly. Even before the arrival of twins, Anita, a nurse, had been hired as live-in help. She rapidly had become more than a paid employee; she had become a member of the family.

Clara now had to break the news to Laurie and Kim that Anita was never coming back from her walk. The girls lined up in front of her, both sets of eyes looking into her eyes. Clara's mouth went dry, and when she opened it, nothing came out.

"Something bad happened to Anita, didn't it?" whispered Laurie.

"Did she get hit by a car?" Kim asked, her face crinkling up.

"Maybe she just got lost and we need to go find her? Is that it?"

Clara opened her mouth again, but before she said a word, the bedroom door opened, and Mitch stood in the doorway.

"Oh, Clara, it's you! Thank goodness you came. We could hear voices coming from this room, and we had no idea who was with the girls."

He stretched out both arms and swept the girls up in a bear hug. "Come with me. Your Aunt Molly and I have something to tell you."

He looked at Clara. "Will you stay a bit? After Molly and I talk to the girls, I'll send them back to you."

"Is Molly all right?" asked Clara.

"No, she's not, but we've gotten through the worst part. I don't think she has any tears left."

After Mitch and the girls disappeared into the master bedroom, Clara had to put her hands over her ears to shut out the howling coming from that room. The girls were taking the news very hard. She wondered how Mitch and Molly were breaking the news to them; she really needed to know. Were they telling them that Anita had been murdered? That would be a very harsh explanation for girls so young. Maybe they just told them that Anita had died.

Mitch had asked Clara to wait until he brought the girls back, but one look at her watch told her it was time to get the van back to the fire station; the boys needed to be taken home.

She was wondering how she was going to handle the situation when the door opened, and Mitch and the girls walked into the room; both girls were carrying backpacks.

When Clara raised her eyebrows in question, Mitch cleared his throat.

"Clara, we need your help. Molly is exhausted from crying."

"Mitch, you know I want to help. That's why I'm here," Clara assured him. "What do you want me to do?"

"The babies seem to sense that Molly's upset."

"Wait a minute. You aren't going to suggest that I take over the care of the twins, are you? I really don't thi…"

"No, no!" Mitch interrupted. "We aren't asking for help with the twins. However, Laurie and Kim need to be in a happier place. Molly and I thought that since the girls get along so well with your three boys and Lucky, spending the night at your house might be the best solution to the problem."

Clara wanted to help, but adding two more charges to her care was not what she had expected. Her mind was whirling: sleeping arrangements, food to feed them, activities to keep them occupied, and school. What about school tomorrow? No, that wasn't a problem because tomorrow was Saturday. But what about the office? Someone had to keep Allen Real Estate open, and it sure wouldn't be Molly who would do it.

Mitch waited a moment for a reply. "I can see you're hesitating. If you really don't want to do this, we'll understand."

"No, no! I want to do it! I was just thinking of all the details involved. Joe and I have more or less solved our problems of who does what on which day. For example, he has Lucky and the three boys at the station. I need to get back there with the van to take the three boys home, but that leaves Joe with Lucky."

"So today is Joe's day to walk Lucky home?" chuckled Mitch. "That dog!"

"That dog is causing a lot of difficulty! Life would be a lot easier without him, that's for sure."

Laurie's lips quivered. "You sound like you don't love Lucky anymore."

Kim's eyes filled with tears. "Lucky's gonna feel so bad when he finds out that you don't love him!"

"No, there I go with my big mouth again!" Clara declared. "I didn't say I didn't love him anymore, but life would be a lot simpler if he'd get into a car. However, Joe pointed out today that if he did get into the car, there would just be another problem; there wouldn't be room for anyone else!"

The girls brightened up. Laurie grinned and Kim giggled.

"That's a funny thing to think about," said Laurie. "What you need is a big dog house hooked to your car. Maybe Lucky just doesn't like to be shut up in something as little as a car."

Clara's mouth dropped open. "I do believe you have a winning idea, Laurie! Come on! Let's go to the station so you can tell Dave about your idea. He's usually building something in the back of the station."

Joe's best friend, Dave, was also a fireman. He was the one who had taught Lucky special tricks using really dead-smelling treats for motivation. Lucky, who had walked Clara down the aisle, had stolen the show at their wedding when he performed a few of his tricks. Using the smelly treat as a signal, Lucky had stood up on his hind legs when the minister asked, "Who gives this woman away?" and barked two times. That was the closest Dave could get Lucky to say, "I do." Wanting another treat, he'd once again stood on his hind legs at the end of the ceremony. His head was level with Clara when the minister said to Joe, "You may kiss your bride," Joe closed his eyes, leaned over, and kissed Lucky on his furry cheek. Joe was still being teased about that little incident.

The ride to the fire station was quiet. The girls, whose mood had momentarily brightened, once again became pensive. They had loved Anita. Clara hesitated to say anything because Mitch hadn't told her how they had explained Anita's death to the girls.

Upon arriving at the station, the girls raced off to the back in search of Dave.

"Hello, there!" he called out to them. "Coming to visit me?"

"Laurie has an idea!" exclaimed Kim.

"Laurie does? Well, let's hear it."

Clara was trying to explain why she had arrived at the station with the girls, but Joe's attention was on the animated conversation between Dave and Laurie. Laurie was gesturing wildly with her arms; Dave was laughing.

"What's she telling him?" he asked Clara.

"She came up with the idea of building a doghouse-trailer of some sort for Lucky to ride on."

Joe thought about it for a moment, and then he nodded his head. "You know, it just might work! If nothing else, the project will keep Dave out of mischief for a while." Joe hadn't completely forgiven Dave for making the wedding so entertaining. The people who had attended it were still laughing.

The girls came running back.

"He liked my idea!" beamed Laurie.

"Dave said he was going to surprise us!" chimed in Kim.

"Well, all I can say about Dave and his surprises…."

Slapping Joe on the back, Clara laughed. "Come on, Joe! You've got to admit that some of his surprises are pretty good."

Joe snorted. "That's easy for you to say."

"Get over it, Joe! It happened! But it's getting late. I should take the kids home, and you and Lucky need to start walking before it gets too dark. By the way, where is that dog?"

"I haven't seen him since you got here. I don't see Billy, either. Where can they have gone? Oh, I see them…."

Joe stopped talking and started running. What he was looking at was a parent's nightmare. A heavy-set young man in a rumpled suit was holding out a piece of candy, trying to coax Billy to come closer.

"Billy! Step back!"

The startled man looked up to see the uniformed captain of the fire department running towards him. Swiftly assessing the situation, the man turned and ran. With one woof, Lucky tore out of the station after him; Joe wasn't far behind. The door of a parked black car opened, and the running man jumped in as it turned onto the street. Joe skidded to a stop. Dark tinted windows made it almost impossible to see the features of the car's occupants. As the car sped past him, he tried but failed to read the mud-smeared license plate.

"What was all that about?" puffed Clara, catching up with Joe.

"I think that man was trying to take Billy!" Joe turned to his son. "Billy, what did that man say to you?"

Billy was embarrassed. He knew he wasn't supposed to talk to strangers, but dinnertime was long past and his stomach was empty. That piece of candy just happened to be his favorite and he was *so* hungry.

"Well?" prompted Joe.

"Aw, Dad, I wouldn't have gone with him! Honest. I just wanted that candy."

"Did he ask you to go with him?"

"He said he had a whole bag of candy that he would share with me if I'd just walk with him to his car."

"I've seen that man before," Clara broke into their conversation. "He and another man had just stepped into Allen Real Estate when Mitch stuck his head in the door and yelled that Anita had been murdered. Things got confusing after that, but I do believe they just left."

"Well, no matter who he is, he was up to no good, that's for sure."

"Thank God we were looking for Billy! A few more minutes and we would have been too late." Clara hugged Billy.

"Am I in trouble?" he asked timidly.

"You boys are in for another lecture when I get home. I don't like what I saw you do, Billy. If that man had gotten his hands on you …." His voice trailed off, horrifying himself with the thought of what just almost happened.

"But, Dad, I'm so hungry!" Billy cried in his defense.

"Everyone is hungry," Clara agreed. "Kids, get into the car. We're stopping for fast-food on the way home!"

That announcement was met with cheers. Encouraged, Clara added, "And you can expect the same for breakfast tomorrow morning."

Five happy kids crawled into the van.

Clara turned to Joe and threw him a kiss. "Have fun on your walk home. The thought of Dave coming up with a trailer to haul Lucky around makes me almost as happy as thinking about the fries I'm going to eat with my burger."

Joe swallowed; his mouth was watering. "Could you bring home something for me? I'm hungry, too. As soon as I make a police report, I'm heading home."

"I know what you usually order, and yes, I will. See ya!"

CHAPTER 6

EMILY GLANCED THROUGH the information her privately hired firm had placed in her hands.

With a worried look on her face, she searched the documents, trying to understand the mystery of the man she had loved and married. There was no record of him before the date that she had met him. It was as if he had been born fully grown at age forty-five. Glancing at the wall behind the desk, she studied the license that declared Mike was a physical therapist, a graduate of the state's university. According to the report in her hands, Mike had never attended the university.

The funeral, scheduled for tomorrow, was a farce. No amount of hysterics on her part had produced any answers to her frantic questions. She had obtained a decorative container that contained his ashes. That container is what would be at the funeral tomorrow.

She wanted to ask someone what was going on, but she had no one.

IN JOE'S BAD dream, he was back in the spider-infested basement of his ex-wife's house. Having nowhere else to go when something Clara had said dashed their wedding plans, he had lived in her creepy basement until the misunderstanding was resolved. The buzzing sound he was hearing confirmed his worst fears: flying spiders.

With a shout and flailing arms, he sat up in bed. Six sets of eyes, ranging in color from blue, hazel, green, to doggy brown, were watching him.

"See," whispered Laurie. "I was right! His eyes *were* twitching!"

"Dad doesn't look too happy," Mackie whispered back. "I told you this wasn't a good idea!"

"But we're hungry!" whimpered Kim.

Breathing hard, Joe flopped back on the bed. He knew he should have some negative feelings about being awakened in such a manner. His own boys had been instructed that the master bedroom was not to be entered if the door was shut. However, the sheer relief that the buzzing was just the kids whispering and not flying spiders put a smile on his face.

"See, he's not mad! He's smiling." Billy cried as he hopped onto the bed; the others followed.

Clara rolled over and groaned. "Joe, what's happening?"

Joe sighed. "Just open your eyes. I'm too tired to describe what's going on."

Clara sat up in bed. "Wow!" she croaked. "I feel like a mother bird. Looks like all my babies have their mouths open waiting for a worm."

"Yuck!" exclaimed Laurie.

"Ugh!" cried Kim.

"Yipp!" barked Lucky.

"Clara's kidding!" Mackie piped up. "She doesn't feed us worms."

"You promised us a fast-food breakfast!" Laurie reminded Clara.

"Coffee, I need coffee!" Clara whimpered.

Joe sighed and swung his legs over the side of the bed.

"I'll make the coffee, but what's this about a promised fast-food breakfast?"

"I have to admit, that's what I promised."

"So get up. Are you going into work today? I have to."

Clara groaned. "Someone has to go to the office and put another sign on the door. Or maybe I can talk one of the mothers into keeping the office open just to answer the phone."

"So I get to walk Lucky back into town this morning?" Joe asked in a flat voice.

"This is what I was talking about! Is Lucky going to be the last straw? Our whole schedule is based around that dog! Arguing over who's going to walk him to work is getting old."

Five pairs of eyes were moving from one speaking person to the other. The sixth pair belonged to Lucky. Hearing his name spoken in a harsh manner was upsetting, He hung his head, and his tail stopped wagging. Had he done something wrong?

"At some point, one of us has got to teach that dog that howling when he's left behind is not acceptable. Other people leave pets at home alone all the time when they go to work. You were just too soft with him when you first got him. That was when you should have trained him."

Clara opened her mouth to say words that she knew she would regret later. Closing her mouth took a lot of effort. She had already paid a big price for making statements without forethought.

"Just go make the coffee, Joe. While you're at it, Lucky needs to be let out."

Turning to the five children still in bed with her, she put a smile on her face. "If we're going out for breakfast, you'd better get dressed! I'm hungry, too."

They scattered to their rooms.

Needing a few minutes of solitude, Clara crawled back under the covers; sleep easily overcame her.

The noise of five kids playing a game of tag finally convinced her that sleep time was over; she had to get up. Thinking that Lucky was still out in the yard, she was surprised that, when she threw her legs over the side of the bed and took a step, she tripped over him. His head was down and his tail wasn't wagging. Feeling his warm nose, Clara became alarmed.

"Lucky, are you ill?"

Lucky lifted his head, gave her a big sigh, and then placed his head back on top of his paws.

"Joe!" yelled Clara. "I think there's something wrong with Lucky!"

"Just what we need! Another straw! I supposed you're going to tell me that now I have to get the fire truck to take him to the vet?"

"You're the captain. You certainly could give yourself permission, don't you think?"

"Clara, the coffee's about done, and I'm getting into the shower," he yelled back. "There's nothing wrong with that dog. He was looking perfectly fine when I let him in. As soon as I get dressed, he and I will start out. Good luck rounding up all your passengers!"

A short time later on their way to the fast-food restaurant, the kids and Clara waved at Joe and Lucky as they drove past. They weren't the only ones waving at the walking pair. Joe, dressed in his captain's uniform and walking a huge black dog, was becoming a familiar sight in the small town. He usually kept the walk at a fast pace, but this morning, Lucky was dragging his feet.

"Come on," Joe urged. "You can walk faster than that!"

Lucky grumbled, looked up at Joe with pleading eyes, and then slowly lowered himself to the ground.

"Whoa!" cried Joe. "What's going on?"

Lucky's answer to Joe's question was to close his eyes.

"Lucky, what are you pulling now? If you think I have a smelly treat to give you, think again."

The dog didn't move.

"Come on!", Joe yelled as he used the toe of his shoe to jiggle the unmoving dog. "Wake up, for heaven's sake!"

What was that noise? Curious, Joe bent over and listened. Lucky was snoring.

"Oh, what next?" Joe muttered as he grabbed his cell phone, wondering whom to call. Clara's attention couldn't be diverted; she was driving a van loaded with kids. Dave. With luck, Dave would already be at the station.

Dave answered on the first ring.

"Hi there, captain! You and Lucky out for your morning walk?" he snickered.

"Enough, already! I'm in trouble and I need help."

"Uh, and what kind of trouble would that be so early in the morning? Does it have anything to do with the police hanging around, waiting for you to show up for work?"

"Police? Oh yeah. I reported yesterday that some man was using candy to lure Billy to his car. I'm surprised it took this long for someone to contact me."

"When did that happen?"

"It happened yesterday, right there at the station. I don't know where you were."

"I was probably in the back working on the project Laurie came up with. I think she has something there. But if your problem is not with the police, what's going on?"

"There's something wrong with Lucky. He just lay down and closed his eyes. I can't wake him up."

"Wow! Right there beside the road?"

"Yes. There are a lot of cars slowing down, wondering what's going on."

"How many men do you think it would take to pick up Lucky? He'll be dead weight."

"I think three of us should be able to lift him onto the truck."

"Hey, captain, I need your permission to drive the truck. And by the way, where are you?"

"Permission granted! We're right outside the town limits. I'll call the vet and tell him we're coming."

"We're on our way."

CHAPTER 7

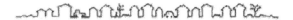

DR. PHILLIP WAS no stranger to the big dog that was showing signs of waking up. Lucky had been in his care after the dog had thrown his body over Joe to protect him from an exploding bomb.

Stroking the dog's newly grown-in fur, the doctor spoke quietly.

"Planning on waking up soon?"

Lucky opened his eyes, gave a big sigh, and then closed them again.

"Are you positive he's going to be all right when he does wake up?" whispered Joe.

"The sleeping pills were fairly strong, but he's a huge dog. He'll feel the effects for a while, but nothing lasting. Have any thoughts about who would have done this?"

Joe shook his head. He had no idea where Lucky had found the sleeping pills. Could someone have thrown the pills over the fence into their backyard? Joe knew Lucky would have been more than happy to devour anything wrapped in meat.

Dr. Phillip observed the man standing beside him. It wasn't too long ago that strange things had been happening to Joe. There had been several attempts on his life, and many not-so-funny occurrences that looked like practical jokes, but weren't. The assaults on Joe had ended suddenly.

"Joe," asked Dr. Phillip, "did you ever find out who was behind all those attacks on you?"

"No, I never did. Clara was sure it had to do with my attempts to find the identity of the boy who had been left in the burning building."

"You never found out anything about him, as I recall."

"That's right. Jerry would be living with someone else right now if I had. Instead, Clara and I adopted him."

"How's that working out? You have two boys of your own, don't you?"

"The two boys are from my first marriage. Billy and Mackie have welcomed Jerry. To be truthful, it's hard not to like Jerry!"

Lucky stirred.

"Looks like sleeping beauty is finally going to wake up," Dr. Phillip observed. "You brought him here on a fire truck. Is that how you'll be taking him home?"

Joe shrugged. "I probably will get some heat from the city fathers for using the station's equipment to haul my dog around, but I can't come up with another solution."

Dr. Phillip grinned. "Good thing you got promoted, Captain!"

GEORGE WING was furious. He knew that his younger brother, Bernard, was a loose cannon, but this was ridiculous. Of course, the story of what he had done hadn't come from Bernard, but from one of George's employees. He had overheard Bernard laughing with Jimmy about their little antic. Jimmy was George's errand boy.

"Tell me, again, about the dog. Why were you angry at him?"

"I have every right to be angry at that dog! He chased me and tried to bite me!"

"Did he bite you?"

"Well...no. But that's only because he didn't catch me."

"So then tell me again what you did to get even. Was that what you were doing? Getting even?"

"Damn straight! That dog needed a lesson, so I wrapped some pills with hamburger meat and threw them over their fence."

"Pills? What kind of pills?"

"Uh, sleeping pills."

"Where in the world did you get sleeping pills? You sure don't need them! You sleep half your life away as it is!"

"In the medicine cabinet."

George jumped up so fast his chair clattered to the floor.

"You used my sleeping pills on the dog?"

"Would you have liked it better if I'd used laxative pills from the other bottle?"

"Oh, for God's sake, Bernard. Now, please tell me why the dog was chasing you in the first place!"

"Do I have to?"

George didn't have to say anything. The look on his face told Bernard the answer.

"I was trying to give a boy a piece of candy. That's all, honest! I didn't touch him."

"What boy?"

"The boy that's connected to that dog, that's who."

"And where did this happen?"

"At the fire station."

George looked at Bernard, and not for the first time, wondered what fickle-finger-of-fate had saddled him with such an albatross for a brother.

"Did anyone get a good look at you before the dog chased you?"

"How should I know?"

"How did you get away?"

"Jimmy."

"Jimmy? How did he get mixed up in this?"

"We were riding around in his car when I seen that cute kid. It was really Jimmy's idea to get him to come to the car so he could get a good look at him."

George shook his head, a look of disgust on his face.

"Bernard, I'm tired of talking to you. The things that you do," George shut his eyes and grimaced. "Hell, I don't even want to think about the things that you do! But, damn it Bernard, my business won't put up with any more of your perverted activities! No more! Did you hear me? No more!"

Bernard's face contorted and tears filled his eyes.

"Don't try pulling that 'I'm being picked-on' attitude, because I'm not buying it. Just remember! One more misstep and both you and Jimmy are out of here! You two will be on your own because I won't be helping you." George shook his head in disgust. "I just hope Mike doesn't get wind of what the two of you did."

Bernard's body jerked. The last time Bernard had seen Mike, he was lying in a ditch, dead.

"You know something that I don't know?" George barked. Bernard never could keep anything hidden.

Bernard snorted. "'Course not!"

"Well, keep it that way. I'm through cleaning up after you. Speaking of Mike, wonder what he's up to? He promised to be in contact with us as soon as we got settled in this town."

Bernard turned his head so his brother couldn't see his face. He felt bad about killing Mike; he'd liked the guy. If only he'd kept his nose out of Bernard's business!

Bernard, who had never voluntarily read a book in his life, had let Mike talk him into going to his wife's book signing at the country club. Knowing that it was a formal event and probably boring, he'd repeatedly turned down the invitation. When Mike dangled the keys to his newly leased red convertible under Bernard's nose, he'd changed his mind.

Looking back, Bernard figured Mike had finagled to get him alone for a reason.

At first, the conversation between the two involved the car's performance and how surprised Emily was going to be. Mike pointed out the unique features of his new acquisition while Bernard put it through its paces. Added to the joy of feeling the warm sun and the wind blowing through his hair, he basked in the attention he was creating as he drove through town waving and honking the horn.

It was when the mood changed and a stern Mike confronted him, not only about his failed attempt to lure a boy to his car, but also about his recently finding Bernard's stash of child pornography pictures that Bernard suddenly remembered a shortcut. The destination of the shortcut was the logging road.

Mike had signed his own death warrant. He never should have threatened to tell George.

CHAPTER 8

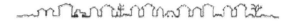

THE U.S. MARSHAL picked up the phone, and then changed his mind. He needed a few more minutes to regain his composure. After blowing his nose and clearing his throat, he again picked up the phone.

"Did you pull the death notice?" he asked the person on the other end of the line.

"It's all been taken care of. All traces of your protected witness have been erased."

"What about his widow? She was a person in the public eye when she was the wife of Senator Mills."

"The press is not touching her with a ten-foot pole. The journalists had been very supportive of the Senator's run for the presidency. When the scandal hit the fan, they felt they had been suckered by him. Looks like they feel that way about his widow, too."

The Marshal sighed. "I shouldn't have allowed him to team up with your fraud investigation. Mike had a mind of his own, though."

"Wonder who it was that figured him out?"

"It must have just happened because I talked to him earlier this week. He never said a word about the possibility of his cover being blown."

"Has this ever happened before?"

"You mean a person in our protective witness program becoming active?"

"Yes. Mike came to me and volunteered. He felt he owed it to his family. I never did hear the whole story."

"It happened at a family reunion. Mike answered the door, so the killer got a good look at him before he started shooting."

"Why was the shooter there in the first place?"

"No one has come up with enough evidence to even investigate. We think the man had been hired to kill a potential whistleblower who was attending a family reunion. The story is that the description he had been given of the mark was so generic, it could have been several people in the room; he just shot everyone."

"Rumors are that he picked the wrong reunion?"

"Rumors are right."

"So our witness was bitter enough to demand permission to go after the group that killed his family? How did he find the group, and why hasn't it been taken down?"

"One of the little players was caught. When he finally talked, he didn't know too much, but he was able to give us a few details about the business. Mike had heard enough to make him think he had found the right group."

"Wouldn't they have recognized him?"

"He'd survived being shot, but most of his face was gone. The plastic surgeons did their best, but his reconstructed face had no resemblance to what he had originally looked like."

"Our guy just got too cocky for his own good!"

"I know, I tried to talk him out of being so public. He went ahead and married that senator's widow, even though we all told him not to. I must admit, the plastic surgeon made him into a different person. His own mother, if she were alive, wouldn't have recognized him if she passed him on the street."

"Well, someone figured out who he was, despite all his changes."

"So you lost your plant and your only witness. Now what?"

"Guess we're back to square one."

"You have no case?"

"No case. Mike was it."

"Mike was supposed to have all the information gathered by this time. What happened?"

"He fell in love is what happened; he got sidetracked."

"I feel bad for his widow. Think how confused she must be. She married someone who really didn't exist. But here's the spooky part: no one in the group knows that he's dead."

"How could they not know? Didn't one of them do it?"

"You'd think so. But he's getting messages on his cell phone."

"What kind of messages?"

"Oh, where are you, why haven't you dropped in like you promised, and why aren't you answering your phone…things like that. They don't seem to have a clue that he's dead."

"Could one of them have done it, and is just keeping his mouth shut?"

"Anything's possible."

Silence

"Could you send in a replacement?"

"Not with a clear conscience. I don't think his shelf-life would be very long. They'd make short work of him, I'm afraid."

"So, who killed Mike?"

CHAPTER 9

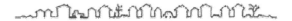

JOE, DEEP IN thought, drove back to the fire station. Maybe Clara was right. As much as they all loved Lucky, he truly was the last straw. The family's activities were difficult enough to schedule without throwing in the idiosyncrasies of a huge dog. Against his better judgment, he knew that he would have to drive the city's fire truck to the vet's office to pick up Lucky. Did he even have a choice? Joe was certain the recently retired Captain Lowell would never have given permission to use the truck for personal reasons.

Joe, immersed in these thoughts, pulled into his reserved parking spot. It was only his quick reactions that allowed him to hit the brakes before he crashed into something already in that space.

"What th…!" he yelled.

Dave came running out, waving his arms.

"Watch where you're going!" he called. "You almost smashed the most ingenious contraption I've ever built!"

"Why did you park it in my space?"

"Because I wanted you to see it! Isn't it glorious?"

Joe got out of his car, walked up to the object, and scratched his head.

Dave had produced an exact replica of the station's truck; no detail had been overlooked.

"By golly, Dave, I think you did it! A miniature fire truck on a trailer! Wow! This is your best work, ever! Now if we can coax Lucky to ride on it, a big problem has been solved! I couldn't believe my ears when Clara talked about getting rid of Lucky because he was making our schedules too hard to follow."

"Aw, come on! Was she really serious?"

"Dave, juggling full time jobs, three boys, and a dog that howls when he's left home alone is enough to make anyone look for a solution. If this contraption works, one huge problem will be eliminated."

"I'd like to take all the credit, but this was Laurie's idea, you know, and it won't work at all if Lucky doesn't cooperate."

Joe laughed. "That dog sure has a mind of his own. I guess that's one of the things that make him special. By the way," Joe asked while pointing, "what's that thing for?"

"That's where his harness will be hooked. He needs to be held securely so that he won't be thrown off if you stop suddenly."

"Good thinking! So to make this work, both Clara and I need trailer hitches put on the back of our vehicles?"

"That should do it," Dave agreed. "How is the dog, by the way? Is he going to be all right?"

"The vet says there shouldn't be any after effects of the sleeping pills. I just wish I knew who would do such a thing."

"When can you pick him up?"

"Any time now. He was wide-awake when I left the vet's. Do you think we can get a hitch on the back of my car in time to go pick him up? I was going to use the fire truck again, but I'd rather not if I don't have to."

"No problem with the hitch. But what if Lucky won't get on our trailer?"

"That's a big possibility. Dave, do you still have that smelly treat that Lucky loves?"

Dave laughed. "Have you forgiven me for using those treats to teach Lucky stupid tricks?"

"I'll forgive you when people quit teasing me."

"Hey, buddy, I never expected that Lucky would stand up on his hind legs without the minister offering him a treat. He did that trick all on his own!"

"Let's go put that hitch on my car. Would you go with me to the vet's in case I have trouble with Lucky? Getting him into that harness might be a problem."

OTHER THAN BEING a bit wobbly on his feet, Lucky walked out of the animal clinic in good shape. Joe slipped a leash on his collar and headed for the parking lot. Lucky's first reaction at the sight of Joe's car was typical; he stiffened his legs and made himself dead weight.

"Easy, old boy, easy. Let's go see Dave. He has a treat for you!"

Lucky could already smell it. Walking to find the source of the smell, he found his buddy, Dave, standing on a familiar truck. Without hesitating, he hopped up on the trailer and took the treat out of Dave's hand.

"So far, so good," Joe said quietly. "How many of those treats did you bring with you?"

"Enough, I hope. Now, I'm going to slip the harness over his head and hook it up."

"Easy does it," whispered Joe.

"Ha! He doesn't seem to mind the harness."

"Dave, do you feel safe riding back there with Lucky? For this trial run, I think you might make the difference between his accepting or not accepting your invention. I promise to go slowly."

"I'll feed him treats the whole way home, and with luck, he won't even know we're moving. Let's go!"

Lucky was so enthralled with the wind blowing in his face that he forgot to eat the smelly treats. Looking back through his rear-view mirror, Joe watched his dog. If dogs could smile, Joe was sure that's what Lucky was doing. After all the years of walking this dog everywhere, the solution had been so simple! He had to remember to thank Laurie.

Clara and the three boys ran out to greet them when Joe pulled into the driveway. The boys were hugging Lucky and Clara was admiring Dave's contraption.

"Dave, you sure do good work!" was all Clara could think to say as she hugged him.

Problem solved. Lucky was no longer the last straw.

CHAPTER 10

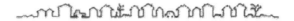

MOLLY AND MITCH held hands as the potential live-in pulled the door closed behind her. Neither one of them said a word until they saw her car pull out of their driveway.

Molly shook her head. "That one wasn't any better than the other twenty we've interviewed."

"Are we being too critical?" asked Mitch. "I know we'll never find anyone as good as Anita, but didn't any of them come close?"

Molly's eyes filled with tears. Anita was gone. To think someone who didn't even know her had decided that she had to die, along with the man in the ditch. The newspapers had at first reported the two murders, but after the initial report, Molly had found no other reference to the man. She had looked for but found no death notice.

Quite a bit of fuss was made over Anita and her funeral. The church had been filled with friends she had made while living with Mitch and Molly. No relatives had shown up for the service.

The mystery of Anita's long walks had been solved when Laurie mentioned that Anita had shared her four-leaf clover dilemma with them. In fact, the two girls had been accompanying Anita on some of those walks. The detective figured that Anita had stumbled over a murder in progress and so had become a part of it. In reading the coroner's report, Mitch had come upon this sentence: *A four-leaf clover was found in the female victim's hand.*

"How many more applicants do we have to interview?" asked Mitch.

"That's all for today, but we have three tomorrow. Will you be around in the afternoon?"

"I'll see to it. You aren't looking so good, hon. I hear you up walking most of the night. Are your restless legs back again?"

"With a vengeance! I have an appointment with my sleep doctor, Dr. Parker, tomorrow morning. I hear the FDA has approved another drug for my problem."

"Good luck with that! Who's watching the twins? I'll be at work."

"Your mother. I haven't asked her before for help, but when I did, she was quite willing."

"Mom had some things to get over before she could jump in and help with our twins. My brother Fred and I were born so close together, raising us was almost like living with twins."

"Your parents must have taken Fred and his wife's death very hard. Dying so suddenly like that in a car accident had to be devastating to both sets of parents."

"My parents handled it better than May's. Her parents wouldn't have anything to do with Laurie and Kim for the longest time. They broke down and cried any time they were around the two kids. Things are better now."

"But back to the problem of replacing Anita. Hopefully, one of the three applicants tomorrow will work out."

———————

ON THE OUTSKIRTS of town, outside a rundown home that housed those who weren't able to take care of themselves, a well-kept-grandmotherly-looking woman stepped out onto the porch to greet her visitor, a tall, scruffy-looking middle-aged man with a five o'clock shadow that was way past that hour. As she tilted back her head in an attempt to look into his eyes, her piled-high white hair threatened to topple. Her steely gray eyes stared into his steely gray eyes.

"About time, Harold! I was beginning to think you'd forgotten about me. Dare I hope this is a loving visit? Just a son checking to make sure his mother was surviving the hell-hole he'd stuck her in?"

"Mom, you know very well why you're here, so don't pull that 'poor mom' shit on me! After that last messed up job, you needed to disappear."

"Couldn't I have disappeared into something nicer? I sure don't like it here! But tell me again, Harold, why I have to apply for that live-in sitter job. You know I hate kids! Can't you find someone else to do it?"

"Quit bellyaching! If you do it right, you won't be there very long."

"That's what you said the last time."

"Give it a rest, Mom!" In a wheedling voice, he added, "How many times do I have to apologize for getting arrested and leaving you hanging?"

"As many times as I want, thank you very much!"

"This time is different. I promise I'll be your good little boy until you get me what I want."

"And tell me again what that is?"

"But I already told you!" He looked closely at his mother. "Are you pulling my leg, or are you getting forgetful in your old age?"

"Just humor me. Tell me again what I'm looking for."

"Aunt Jennie's ring."

"And how am I supposed to find it?"

"You'll be living in Anita's quarters, won't you? I'm sure the Hatch family has no idea that she had a ring worth half a million."

"And do you remember why she gave that ring to your sister Anita and not to you?" she smirked, "Because I sure do!"

A backhanded slap silenced her.

"Mom, any more backtalk and you can walk right back into the house."

Hanging her head to hide defiant eyes, she mumbled, "I'm sorry."

"That's better."

"Tell me what you want to do, and I'll do it. I promise."

"You better. Just keep in mind that I'm still paying for your room here."

She eyed her son with cold eyes. "I can't believe I raised a man like you! After all the things I did …."

"Cut the crap, Mom. We both know what kind of a mother you were."

She snorted. "You had the mother you deserved! But back to this job. You say there are infant twins? I'll be taking care of babies? I hate babies! They cry, poop, and spit up! I had three of my own and I didn't like any of them…certainly not you!"

"Now, isn't that just what a son wants to hear coming out of his mom's mouth?" He spit over the porch rail.

"Well, you weren't very lovable!"

"What about Ted? Was he lovable?"

She sniffed. "That brother of yours has spent most of his life behind bars. But, no, he was the worst of the three of you."

"You used to blame things on me that I never even thought of doing. I kept telling you that it wasn't me, but you never believed me."

"That's because the two of you looked so much alike. I wonder if that's still true," she said with a faraway look in her eyes. "Lord, I can't remember the last time I laid eyes on that child."

There was no softness in Harold's eyes when he asked his mother, "Have you even been in contact with Ted?"

"No. Why should I?"

"So you don't know that he might get a reduced sentence?"

"Ha, if he does, it won't be based on good behavior!"

"Well, there's a chance he might be getting out real soon now. Seems the prisons are too full."

"So, you've been in contact with him? I'll bet you told him about the ring." Seeing the look on Harold's face, she scoffed, "You did, didn't you?"

"Yes, I did. What's so wrong about that?"

"That means he'll be nosing around here, making sure he gets his share of the money when we sell the ring. But back to the job you're sending me on. Do I really have to do it?"

"If the ring is there, it shouldn't take you too long to find it. As soon as you do, you can leave. Call me, and I'll come and pick you up. Don't forget the two girls that live there, too. Their names are Laurie and Kim. Seems they belonged to Mr. Hatch's brother, but he and his wife are dead."

"What if they investigate my past?"

Harold let out a short laugh. "We couldn't let that happen, now could we? I used the identity of your friend, Heather. She died last week with a squeaky-clean record. Now, Heather had been a nurse, so brush up on your nursing skills, and work on the questions and answers I've printed for you."

"Stop right there! I don't think you've thought this thing through. I'm sure her death has been reported! If the Hatch family does any checking, they're going to find that out."

"Who said it was reported?"

She studied her son's face. "What are you saying?"

"What I'm saying, Mom, is just don't ask any questions. This is your story: you lived with your widowed daughter and her children until she recently remarried. Her new husband doesn't like you, so he kicked you out of the house right after he found out that his job was transferring him overseas. Since that leaves you with nowhere to live, you will have to stay in an assisted living home unless the Hatch family hires you."

"Hmmm. That's a pretty good story. Make it up all by yourself?"

Harold hissed, "Watch your mouth, Mom!"

"I wonder why Heather never mentioned she had a daughter. Are you sure there's no one else to go sniffing around asking questions?"

"Yes, I'm sure! Just shut-up and pay attention! Heather had just the one daughter, and with her out of the country, no one will be looking for a death notice. Read what I've written about her background in case they ask you questions, and be sure and answer when they call you Heather or Mrs. Kingham. Mom, people like Heather are cash cows to those who know how to work the system."

"The system?"

"Yeah. Social Security checks, doctor's visits, wheelchairs, prescriptions, medication, x-rays…."

"Oh, I get it. Someone has a scam going? You in on it?"

"No, but I'm hoping. A local guy by the name of George has contacted me. Seems one of his men was found dead in a ditch, and George is looking for a replacement. I would have to do a crash-course in physical therapy, because that's what the dead guy did."

"Wait a minute! That ditch…was it the same ditch that my daughter was in? You want to get involved in a scam that got your sister killed?"

"If you'd read the paper, you'd know that they've established that Anita had no connection to that man. She was just in the wrong place."

"Anita, my lily-white-stick-to-the-rules-daughter." The woman shook her head in wonder. "How did I ever produce one like that?"

"Don't blame yourself. She was bent straight like that when she was born. But let's get back to the business at hand. You are now Heather Kingham."

"Poor Heather. I'm sure she never did anything illegal in her whole life." With a deep sigh she added, "I really miss her; she was my best friend. She depended on me to look after her at the end when she was so sick."

"You looked after her?" He was both surprised and amused. "Me, I wouldn't let you look after anything of mine, not even my goldfish! Oh, wait a minute. You already did that! Remember? I came home from camp one summer and found all my fish floating on their backs...and smelling to high heaven. You hadn't fed them for two weeks."

"I had other things to think about! Now, I want to know what you plan on doing with me after I find the ring. You really aren't going to make me come back to this home, are you? It's full of old people who smell like urine!"

"You just described yourself, Mom."

"Watch your mouth!" she hissed. "I will not come back here! I'm tired of being under your thumb because you kept all the money from the last job. Maybe I'll just keep my sister's ring and..."

From a life spent dodging fists from a drunken husband and two mean sons, the woman had perfected the trick of jerking back her head at the last second. The fist that flew past her jaw smashed into a nail that was sticking out of the porch railing.

With a cry of anguish, Harold crumbled to the floor. Looking down at her son writhing in pain, the prim grandmotherly-looking woman pulled back her leg and delivered a well-placed kick to his groin.

CHAPTER 11

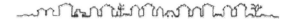

MOLLY AND MITCH held hands as today's second potential live-in pulled the door closed behind her. Neither one of them said a word until they saw her car pull out of their driveway.

Molly shook her head. "That one wasn't any better than the other twenty-two we've interviewed."

"One more to go. We have no more applicants after this one. What do we do then?"

Molly sighed. "I suppose you and I will just have to continue what we've been doing ever since Anita left us. We've managed, haven't we?"

"Molly," Mitch quietly asked as he cupped her face in his hands, "have you looked in the mirror lately?"

Sticking out her tongue, she pulled back from her husband. "I think I look as good as you do! We have a matching set of eye-bags!"

Mitch chuckled. "I'm so tired, I stumble into walls and doorjambs. But you, my dear, are back to walking at night. I get some sleep when the twins sleep, but you don't."

"Dr. Parker hasn't come up with the right combination of drugs to calm my restless legs. No matter how exhausted I am, my damn legs keep screaming at me, 'Move me, move me!' So I walk." She paused, and then added, "I don't have a choice."

"I know you don't. I cringe when I remember back when you were pregnant and couldn't take what you called your 'magic pills'."

Molly stopped him by planting a kiss on his lips. "That's water over the dam, Mitch. Forget it!"

"Forget that you were leaving me before the birth of the twins? I can't forget that, Molly. You tried to tell me, and I wouldn't listen. Back then, I thought that if you loved me enough, you could stay in bed with me. Now, I know better."

"Thanks to Dr. Parker!"

"Yeah, I know. I wouldn't listen to you, but I did listen to Dr, Parker...oh, a taxi just pulled into our driveway!"

Holding hands, they stood in front of the picture window and watched as a tall, slim, modestly dressed elderly woman paid the driver. Walking up to their door was the model of what a grandmother should look like. With her white hair gathered in a bun at the nape of her neck, sensible shoes on her feet, and a warm smile on her face, she waved at the two people who were watching her from within the house.

Molly squeezed Mitch's hand. "Would you look at that? I think we just struck pay dirt!"

"Looks like it!" Mitch grinned as he opened the door.

Standing there was the solution to their problems.

The woman held out her hand, took a deep breath, and hesitated for just a heartbeat. What was that name, again? Oh, yes....

"Hello, I'm Heather Kingham, here to apply for the advertised position."

Almost forgot my new name! Can't have that, she thought as she studied the two people who were welcoming her. Redheaded-green-eyed Mrs. Hatch was small, probably just making it to five feet, if that. Mr. Hatch, on the other hand, was tall, blond, and blue-eyed. If there were kids in this house, she sure didn't see them, but something had caused both parties to have black-circled eyes.

Is that how I'm going to end up looking if they turn the kids over to me? Not if I find... what is it that I'm supposed to find?

Her train of thought was interrupted when Mrs. Hatch held out her hand in welcome. Oh, well, later she'd remember what she was supposed to find. But first, she had to convince these two people they should hire...what was that name again?

CHAPTER 12

OFFICER TOM ALLEN finally caught up with Detective Mitch Hatch at the Omelet Shop where Mitch was eating breakfast.

"Finally!" Tom grunted as he sat down on the stool besides Mitch. "I've been trailing after you for days!"

"I've been busy with several things, the double murder being just one of them. Sorry about sitting at the counter. All the tables were full, and I didn't have time to wait for one."

"Stools are fine, but there's not much privacy here," Tom muttered. Along the counter, heads were turned in their direction, trying to listen to what a police officer and a detective had to talk about.

Mitch was buttering the last piece of toast when he remembered something. "Tom, Molly will have my head if she finds out I ran into you and didn't ask about Marie. How's she doing?"

"Depends on the time of day when you ask her. She switches from glowing to barfing at warp speed! I've never seen anything like it."

"Is she still working at the hospital?"

"Part-time. She's carrying so much weight that her legs are complaining. The doctor prescribed elastic stockings that she has to put on before getting out of bed in the morning. That's fun to watch!"

"Just think! Molly's little brother will soon be a dad."

"Can't happen soon enough to suit me. I'd like to have my wife back!"

Mitch laughed. "I hate to tell you this, buddy, but this is the calm before the storm. Just wait until your little junior appears. You aren't going to get your wife back anytime soon, believe me!"

Tom sighed. "I miss her," he said quietly.

Mitch nodded. "I know the feeling."

The two sat in silence.

"I'm finished," Mitch declared as he picked up the bill. "Just let me settle up here, and then I'll walk back to the station with you."

The sun was shining brightly on the little western Michigan town, the water on the big lake was shimmering in different shades of blue, and the people who passed them on their walk called out friendly greetings.

Tom shook his head. "I don't like to think that in this town there's someone who tried to take Billy."

"I don't either, but it happened. Thank God Joe was there to stop it!"

"There were two of them. Joe saw the one who was offering the candy run to a black car with tinted windows, and a license plate with mud smeared over it. Clara claims he and another man had been in her office the day you stuck your head in looking for Molly. Since Molly had been in the office when the men dropped in, she saw the guys, too."

"Does Clara know why the two men were in her office?"

"No, because after you yelled that Anita had been murdered, according to Clara, they just disappeared."

"Hmmm. Maybe they were looking for something to buy or rent? If so, I think we'd better check with the other real estate offices in town. If they ended up buying or renting something, we could track them down."

They were almost to the station when Tom asked Mitch, "Why were you eating breakfast at the Omelet Shop? I thought your new live-in help would be cooking for you."

"Ah, you would think so, wouldn't you? But you wouldn't wonder if you ever ate one of Mrs. Kingham's breakfasts."

"That bad?" grinned Tom.

"That bad. I didn't know you could mess up toast, but she can. I don't even want to think about what she does with eggs!"

"Come on! How can anyone mess up eggs?"

"She does. Yesterday she jellied my pancakes and poured syrup on my eggs." Mitch paused, a thoughtful look on his face, and then added, "Come to think of it, it was quite a tasty breakfast!"

"Tasty enough to be on the Omelet Shop's menu?" teased Tom.

Mitch poked Tom with his elbow. "Not likely!"

The two men walked quietly for a bit before Mitch picked up the conversation. "Laurie and Kim don't like her," he said softly, almost as if he were talking to himself.

"What? Did I hear you say something about Laurie?"

In a stronger voice, Mitch replied, "I just said that the girls don't like Mrs. Kingham."

"Well, Anita's shoes are pretty hard to fill. Maybe they just resent that someone is trying to take Anita's place?"

"That's what I thought, too. Well, at the beginning, I did."

"Something happen that changed your mind?"

Mitch shrugged. "It could be nothing, but Laurie has a bruise on her upper arm."

"So?" Tom's red eyebrows danced.

"It was the funny look she gave me when I asked her about it."

"Nothing more? What does a funny look from an eleven-year-old look like?"

"It's just that the girls have always been so open with me. The three of us were connected by grief after the accident; I'd lost a much loved brother, and they'd lost both their parents."

"Are you saying they're acting differently toward you?"

"Not just me because Molly has noticed it too. It's like they're hiding something from us," Mitch explained as the two arrived at Tom's station.

"Then it's a good thing you're a detective, Mitch. You'll just have to figure out what's going on in your own house."

"Right now I have to find out what those two guys were doing in Molly's office. I'll spend the rest of the day checking with the other real estate offices in town. Maybe those two showed up in one of them."

"Keep me in the loop." Tom waved as he entered the station.

CHAPTER 13

"WHAT'S SHE DOING now?" Laurie whispered as she struggled to stay upright while supporting the weight of Kim on her shoulders.

"Quit jiggling! I'm gonna fall off!" hissed Kim.

"Well, you're moving around and I can't keep balanced. What's she doing now?"

"She's going through Anita's desk."

"Ouch, you're pulling my hair!"

"Stand still!"

"I'm trying! What do you mean, going through? What's she doing?"

"She's dumping drawers. She looks at the dumped stuff, and then she dumps another one. Boy, is she gonna have a mess to clean up!"

"She's looking for something…oh…quick, get down! Someone just came out of the house!"

Mitch rounded the corner and came to an abrupt stop when he saw his two nieces rolling around on the grass. "Oh, there you are! I've been looking for you two."

Looking embarrassed, the two girls untangled themselves and got up. "Well, we're right here, Uncle Mitch! We were just playing a game, weren't we Kim?"

Kim nodded. "Yes, just a silly game."

Mitch gave them both a suspicious look. Were the bruises coming from playing a rough game? Something was going on with these two, but now was not the time to figure what it was.

"I was looking for you because I think you'd like to see who came to visit!"

"We have visitors?" squeaked Kim.

"Yes, a special visitor at that! Laurie, you had a big hand in this visit."

"I did?" Laurie's eyes were big.

Those were the last words that came out of her mouth before a black streak came sliding around the corner, knocking her down and holding her immobile.

"Lucky!" she cried. "How did you get here?"

The dog answered with a deep chest rumble and a kiss.

"Lucky, where are you?" called Clara as she rounded the corner of the house. "Oh, there you are!"

Lucky raised his head and gave Clara a doggy smile.

"Is this your way of thanking Laurie for her idea?"

"My idea?" Laurie squealed as she tried to push the dog off. "Did Dave really make the trailer I told him about?"

"He sure did, Laurie! Lucky loves his new fire truck! We've spent the day visiting places we never could walk to. Come on! You've got to see Dave's creation!"

The entire Hatch household was gathered around the fire truck replica when the front door opened, and Mrs. Kingham stepped out.

"Come join us," Mitch called to her.

Mrs. Kingham surveyed the group, her eyes landing on the huge dog that had jumped onto what looked like a small fire truck. She was puzzled why the group was making a big fuss over the fact that the dog had gotten on the thing. What was so wonderful about that? Isn't that what dogs do? They jump. Her dislike for dogs was right up there along with her dislike for children.

Reluctantly, she closed the door behind her, and grasping the railing, descended the porch steps. Waiting to meet her was a small pretty woman, a tall black-haired man, and three young boys. The names of Joe, Clara, Billy, Mackie, and Jerry rattled around in her head. Since she wouldn't be around long enough to ever see them again, she made no effort to put names to the faces.

Mitch was watching his two nieces as Mrs. Kingham approached the group. The two of them, holding hands, were backing away. He found that troubling.

Clara looked at the elderly woman with critical eyes. So this was Anita's replacement? To hire someone this old, they had to be desperate. Polite words of welcome were said, the fire truck replica was admired, and then Clara announced, "Time to go! Joe is dropping me off at the bookstore."

"Yeah!" Jerry informed them. "We get to eat ice cream while we wait for her!"

Molly turned to Clara. "Buying a book?"

"No, I already bought and read the first book in a series written by Senator Mill's widow. Today she's having a book signing and I'm going to stand in line and see if she'll sign mine even though I didn't buy it from that store."

"Didn't she remarry shortly after the senator died?"

"Yes, she married Mike Fuller. Remember, the other body in the ditch with Anita? No one really knows the details behind the two deaths because, for some reason, there were none. Poor woman! She was inconsolable for a time, but now it looks like she's back to writing."

Goodbyes were said, Lucky was strapped into his harness, and the happy family drove away. The last straw that had threatened to ruin a perfectly constructed schedule threw back his head, enjoying the breeze that ruffled his fur and made his ears flop.

The line to have a book autographed was long. Taking her place at the end, Clara viewed the row of people patiently waiting their turn. Did she really want to do this? The rest of her family was eating ice cream, and here she was standing....

Off to Clara's right was a man trying to get the attention of the author. When Emily Mills Fuller raised her head and saw who it was, she smiled and waved back. Clara's breath caught in her throat. The waving man was someone she had seen before. He was one of the men who had been in the office the day of Anita's murder, and he was also the one who had offered Billy candy. All thoughts of leaving and joining the ice cream party disappeared. If it took an hour, she knew she had to stay in line. When it was her turn to have her book signed, she'd ask the author about that man.

The line moved slowly. Most people had things to say to Emily, and some even told her what they wanted her to write in their book. By the time Clara had worked her way to the front of the line, to her disappointment, Emily stood up and stretched.

"Time for a break!" she said, massaging her right hand. "I've got writer's cramp!"

"Oh, please," Clara begged. "I won't ask you to sign my book if you'll answer just one question!"

Emily looked annoyed as she viewed the woman in front of her. Thinking she was another writer who couldn't finish a story, she turned and walked away without making a comment.

"It's about that man who waved to you…" Clara called after her.

"You talking about Bernard?" Emily halted mid-step and turned to face Clara.

"If that's the name of the man who waved at you, then, yes, I'm talking about Bernard."

"What makes you ask? He's new in town."

"He was in my real estate office," replied Clara, relieved that Emily was talking with her.

"Was there another man with him?"

"Yes, there was. He looked older than Bernard."

"That's because he's Bernard's older brother. The other man is George Wing. George owns some kind of medical company." About to enter a room, she paused to add, "My late husband, Mike, worked for him."

The restlessness of the boys had Joe thinking this whole arrangement had been a bad idea. With nothing else to do after they'd finished their ice cream, he was about to go to the signing, find Clara, and then talk her into dropping the whole project, when Lucky's welcoming 'woof' announced her arrival.

"Let's see!" yelled Mackie. "I wanna see what the lady wrote!"

"Me first!" chimed in Billy as he pushed his older brother away.

"Hey, you guys, settle down! There's nothing to see. She didn't write in my book," Clara admitted as she crawled into the car.

Turning to Clara, Joe remarked, "A whole hour and you have nothing to show for it?"

"Yes, a whole hour, and yes, I do have something to show for it. I have information!"

"Information about what? Let's hear it!"

Clara glanced into the back of the van where Billy sat along with Mackie and Jerry. They had tried not to make a big deal out of the candy incident. Joe had given them a stern lecture about strangers, but they hadn't dwelled on what might have happened if Billy had been snatched.

"I'll tell you when we get home, Joe. Don't push, okay?"

He hesitated but a moment. Clara usually knew the right thing to do, so he nodded his head. He would wait until they were home to find out what information she had picked up at the book signing.

After harnessing Lucky securely to his own fire truck and making sure the three boys were buckled-up, the entire family rode away in style; no one would ever again have the lonely job of walking Lucky home.

Joe and Clara, held captive by their tight schedule, were not able to have a private conversation until dinner was prepared and eaten, schoolwork was finished and inspected, baths were drawn and supervised, prayers were composed and recited, and three boys were kissed and tucked into bed…but not before a favorite story was read.

Joe looked at Clara's droopy eyes. "Love, do you have any energy left at all? If you want to wait until tomorrow to tell me what information you picked up at the book signing, I suppose curiosity won't kill me…but then, again, it might! Do you want to take that chance?" he teased as he hugged her.

Clara stepped closer, laid her head on his shoulder, and closed her eyes. "If you'd just stand still and talk a little softer, I could take a short nap right here."

"On my shoulder? I don't think so!" he laughed as he pushed her away. "Come on. Let's talk about it in bed."

Joe leaned his head back against the bed's headboard and closed his eyes. "So the two men in your office were George Wing and his brother, Bernard. George has some kind of medical business, and Mike Fuller, the other dead person in the ditch, worked for him. Bernard is the guy who tried to entice Billy with candy."

In a voice that was muffled by a downy comforter, Clara remarked, "I know other real estate offices have been contacted. Did that lead anywhere?"

"No. If they're living in this area, they found the house or apartment on their own."

"So where does that leave us?"

Joe yawned. "That leaves us with a name. We'll tell Detective Mitch that we know who tried to pick up Billy. It's too late to call him now, so let's wait until tomorrow morning. Okay?"

Joe's question was answered by a light snoring sound coming from a fast-asleep Clara.

"Thanks for agreeing with me, hon," he whispered as he snuggled up to his new wife.

Exhausted as he was, Joe was still anxious for morning to come. Just thinking about the surprise he was going to spring on Clara at breakfast made him smile. He had worked hard at keeping the arrangements a secret; Clara didn't have a clue. Mrs. Haver, Jerry's former foster mother, had happily consented to take all three boys, and since Lucky was no longer restricted in his travels, he was going to spend time with the Hatch family. Molly and Mitch agreed that, if it meant the newlyweds would finally have a delayed honeymoon, the big dog was more than welcome.

That left Joe and Clara free of responsibilities for the first time since their wedding.

CHAPTER 14

HESTER...HAZEL...that doesn't sound right. What was the name of my friend? Oh yes, Heather. Why do I have so much trouble remembering that? And why am I here in the park? I must have something more important to do than sit here on a bench, doing nothing. I should be looking for...ah...a ring. Yes, that's it, I'm supposed to find a ring.

Laurie and Kim, from atop the park's jungle gym, were watching Lucky chase a squirrel. Having the big dog all to themselves was bringing laughter back into their lives, a sound that had been missing since Anita's death. The look on Lucky's face when the squirrel got away again, was sending them into fits of giggles. Early in the game, the squirrel had realized that the big black thing was too slow to catch him. Laurie's gaze left Lucky and glanced in the direction of Mrs. Kingham and the twins. She poked Kim. "She's doing it again. Watch her lips...they're moving. She talking to herself."

Rubbing her upper arm where Mrs. Kingham had pinched her, Kim glared in the woman's direction. "She's a mean old lady, that's what she is!"

They watched as Mrs. Kingham got to her feet and walked away, leaving the twins behind in their double stroller.

"Would you look at that!" Laurie exclaimed.

"Where's she going?"

"Looks like she's going home!"

"B-b-but the twins!"

As they watched, the retreating Mrs. Kingham abruptly stopped walking. Slowly, as she turned around, the vacant expression on her face changed to one of awareness. She hurriedly returned to the bench.

"What was all that about?" Kim asked.

"I don't know! But it sure looked like she was leaving."

"Isn't she supposed to be watching us?"

Laurie didn't answer immediately. "Kim, I think there's something not right about Mrs. Kingham."

"You mean besides her pinching us?"

Laurie nodded.

"Are we going to tell Uncle Mitch?"

"I wouldn't know what to tell him, Kim. We think she's looking for something, but we can't prove it. When Molly's at work, we know that Mrs. Kingham ignores the twins. She doesn't change their diapers until just before Molly gets home from work, but if we tell on her, it would be our word against hers. We *do* know she doesn't like us! That's one thing we can prove by our black-and-blue pinch marks."

"Well, we saw her walk away. We could tell Uncle Mitch that."

"She could explain that she just took a little walk to stretch her legs, or something like that. It would make us look dumb."

"So we're not going to do anything?"

"I didn't say that. Uncle Mitch is a detective; he figures out things. I think that's what we should do."

"Like playing a game?" squealed Kim. "I love playing games!"

"It's more than a game, but yes, we can pretend it's a game. But no one can know what we're doing."

"No one?"

"Especially Mrs. Kingham. She might do more than just pinch us."

———

THUNDER AND LIGHTENING woke Kim and Laurie. It was Saturday morning, and Molly had agreed to a play-date requested by the mother of two girls the same ages as Kim and Laurie.

"Kim, do you hear what I hear?" Laurie called to Kim whose bed was positioned beside a window.

"Yeah. I hear and I can see. There are big puddles out there. I'll bet this means no play-date for us."

"Shoot. That means we have to put up with Mrs. Kingham all day."

"I suppose we don't have a choice."

Lucky, who had spent the night on the floor between the beds, yawned.

Kim giggled. "I think we just woke Lucky. He probably has to go out and do his thing. Remember, we promised Molly and Mitch we'd keep the yard clean. Ugh."

"And we will! I really like having him around, don't you?"

Kim sighed. "Lucky is wonderful. I wish we could have our own dog, but what are the chances we'd get one as special as he is?"

Lucky not only had gone back to sleep, his deep breathing had a rumble to it, sounding much like a snore.

Laurie reached out a hand and patted his head. "It sounds like he went back to sleep."

"I think he has the right idea!" yawned Kim.

With sighs of contentment, the girls burrowed under the covers. Soothed by the sound of pounding rain, they were almost asleep when their bedroom door flew open and Mrs. Kingham burst into their room.

"Get up, you lazy girls! You're going to be late for school!"

"Wha…?" cried Laurie, sitting up in bed.

"You heard what I said! Now get up and get dressed!"

"Mrs. Kingham, it's Saturday! There's no school today."

"Don't give me that story, missy, I know what day it is! You can't pull that old trick on me. My own kids used to try it!"

"But it *is* Saturday!" argued Kim.

"Don't you sass me!" With her pinching hand outstretched, Mrs. Kingham rushed at Kim.

Lucky growled.

Molly appeared in the doorway. "What's going on in here?"

Mrs. Kingham quickly pulled back her hand; she'd forgotten about the damn dog. "I'm just trying to get the girls up so they won't be late for school," she said, smiling sweetly.

"Mrs. Kingham, today is Saturday."

"Oh!" was all Mrs. Kingham could think to say.

At breakfast, Kim asked, "What do we do now? We were planning on going to the park, but that's out. What else were we going to do with those other girls?"

"Besides watching them play with Lucky? That's why they were coming, you know."

"Yeah, I know. Besides that, what were we going to do?"

"We were going to play dress-up."

"Wanna play dress-up anyway?"

"I suppose we could. We haven't played that since Anita...."

The girls didn't have a word that they felt comfortable saying when speaking of Anita. *Dead* was hard, and *murder* was almost impossible to think about.

"That morning, right before she went on that last walk, she threw some of her old stuff into our dress-up basket. We were going to play when she got back."

Laurie's eyes filled with tears. Pushing her cereal bowl away, she left the table.

"I don't know if I can do it," she sobbed. "I don't know if I can put on one of Anita's dresses...oh, how I miss her! It hurts to think about her."

"But I like to think about her," Kim said softly. "She's gone, but I don't want to forget her. I don't think she'd want that."

Laurie blew her nose. "I don't think she'd want that, either. I changed my mind. Let's go see what she put into the basket."

"We can dress in her old clothes and talk about all the good times we had with her. She loved to play dress-up with us!"

Laurie giggled. "I have an idea! Let's dress up Lucky!"

Since Molly had gone into work for a few hours, Mrs. Kingham felt free to disregard the crying twins who were being held captive in an oversized playpen. In the past, she'd found that if she ignored them long enough, they'd cry themselves to sleep. What she wanted to do was to check on the girls who were playing dress-up. The clothes, she'd been told, had belonged to Anita.

The first thing she saw was Lucky. Looking extremely uncomfortable, he sported a bonnet on his head and a shawl draped over his back. Dumb dog; she was looking forward to the end of his visit.

Kim, dressed in a red jumpsuit with the pants legs rolled up, was wearing a necklace and earrings she had found in the basket, along with a pair of high-heeled shoes. Mrs. Kingham actually experienced a twinge that felt suspiciously like motherly love as she watched Kim clomping around the room in Anita's castoffs. Her daughter had been such a disappointment! She could have been an asset in the family's business if only she'd stuck around. However, when a very young Anita had discovered just what the family business entailed, she was appalled.

It was when Kim did a dramatic fling of her hands that Mrs. Kingham saw it. The ring, too large for Kim's finger, was stuck on her thumb. Mrs. Kingham's eyes widened as she watched Kim's flinging arm send an empty juice glass flying through the air, along with the ring that had escaped her thumb.

Before she could scoop up the ring that lay in the middle of smashed glass, Molly, who had just returned from work, ran into the room.

"Don't move, any of you! No, Kim, put that piece of glass down! I don't want anyone getting cut. Get Lucky out of the room!" With that, Molly ran to the garage, and when she returned, she was pulling an industrial vacuum.

Pushing aside Mrs. Kingham, who was on her knees searching through the pieces, Molly scolded. "Mrs. Kingham, I don't want you to get cut, either! So move!"

Mrs. Kingham reluctantly stood up and stared in dismay as Molly, after picking up the big pieces, vigorously vacuumed the floor. Horrified, she watched the shattered glass, along with the ring, being sucked into the vacuum bag.

"Thank goodness the twins are asleep in their pen! I don't want them crawling in this room until I get every piece of glass off the floor!"

"Aunt Molly, I'm sorry," cried Kim. "I didn't mean to break that glass!"

"It's all right, Kim. Those glasses are from the dollar store."

Molly stopped her inspection of the floor when a strange noise coming from Mrs. Kingham made her glance in her direction. Mrs. Kingham, clutching her heart, was opening and closing her mouth, much like a fish out of water.

Kind-hearted Molly was touched. "Mrs. Kingham, relax. Nothing bad happened here; it was just an accident! Don't look so concerned!"

A high piercing sound came out of Mrs. Kingham mouth as she ran from the room.

CHAPTER 15

BERNARD HAD A worried look on his face when he asked, "What do you mean, we're going to another town?" His brother George had just announced that they'd be moving out of the hotel room where they had been living.

"Thanks to you and your perverted ways, we can't stay here," George replied not too kindly.

Bernard knew he was guilty, but it never hurt to claim innocence. "I didn't do nothing!"

"You call trying to lure a four-year-old boy with a piece of candy nothing? My God, Bernard! Our poor mother would be rolling around in her grave if she knew what you and Jimmy do! Come to think of it, I can't stand to think of it, either!"

Bernard had the grace to blush.

"No, we have to go to another town, and be quick about it. I have spies, you know. Seems a detective visited all the real estate offices in town, trying to find if one of them rented or sold us a house. They want to find us, Bernard, and we can't let that happen. Two people in that Allen Real Estate office know what we look like, and according to my spies, one of those ladies saw you when you were doing that little candy trick with the young boy."

"They might have seen me, but they don't know who I am, do they?"

"I don't know the answer to that, and I'm not inclined to stick around to find out that you're wrong. Anyhow, I have my eye on several nursing homes so you and I will be traveling for the next couple of weeks."

"Ugh," Bernard wrinkled his nose, "Tell me I don't have to go in any of those places! Those old geezers freak me out!"

"Bernard, you're just looking at them through the wrong set of eyes. View them as a potential source of income! Even their pee smells better when you connect that smell to money…lots of money!"

"I wish you'd forget about the old people and just get more doctors, physical therapists, and pharmacists into the scam. Sending phony patients to them just seems like a less complicated way to make money than to mess around with old coots."

"Get over it, Bernard. I wish you were more interested in the family business. We lost a good man when Mike died. I'd replace him with you if I thought you could do it, but your heart just isn't in it."

Bernard flinched, remembering the feel of the gun in his hand. Keeping his face blank, he asked, "Are the police making any headway into the murders?"

"Don't seem to be, and what surprises me is the lack of police investigation. More information came out about that lady than about Mike. It's as if he wasn't important enough to even bother with finding who murdered him. Mike was a good guy!"

Bernard swallowed the bile in his throat that was fighting its way upward. "I really liked Mike. Have you found his replacement?"

"I've had one interview with a man by the name of Harold. I'm considering him, depending on how much effort he puts into becoming a believable physical therapist. He and his mother have a record of several successful frauds and scams. His mother has been involved in all of his schemes, but she must be pretty old by now."

Bernard pulled out his suitcase and started emptying drawers. "Any idea where we're headed?"

"We'll figure that out once we get out of this town."

———————

HIS PLATE WAS heaped with the most expensive item on the restaurant's menu, and his champagne glass was full, but Bernard's regret that he had accepted the dinner invitation was growing. Across the table he watched George beaming at tonight's patsy. With eyes burning with passion, George had the appearance of a saint on a mission to save the man's soul.

Bernard knew better. The passion in George's eyes had nothing to do with saving the man's soul; the gleam in his eye was greed. With a little persuasion, tonight's pawn would be added to his growing network of health providers.

For two weeks the brothers had traveled, visiting nursing and assisted living homes. After three days of accompanying his brother into the homes, Bernard had revolted; he refused to get out of the car. It was clear to him that the people living in these homes felt the same way he did; they didn't want to be there, either. He was surprised that he, a murderer, could have such repugnant feelings toward the family business that profited on the backs of these poor souls. George sometimes arranged to buy the home they visited, other times he just lined up the professionals who worked there. Tonight's mark would become part of a team that shifted patients to participating doctors, pharmacists, and therapists for unneeded services.

Bernard was learning more about the family business than he ever wanted to know. He listened while George described to their dinner guest how easy the road to wealth would be if he agreed to become part of the team. When George detected a shadow of doubt in the man's eye, he casually mentioned the perks that would be his if he joined:

yacht trips, a journey to an exotic part of the world to hunt and fish, cruises, and because the man had mentioned his three children, George threw in a family vacation at Disney World. It made Bernard feel embarrassed just watching the guest's eyes light up with anticipation.

George continued to explain what was expected of a team member. Not only would the new recruit refer work to participating health providers for a kickback, he would order unnecessary equipment, he would "hard code" a service to put it into a higher category for greater reimbursement, and he would order services that weren't medically needed.

The recruit had one last question. "What if I get caught?"

Bernard blew off that concern with a wave of his hand. "Been there, done that," he grinned.

"And you're still here?"

"Nothing to it! Twice I've had my Medicare license revoked, but since no one from the government showed up at the appeal hearings, my license was reinstated...both times"

The man looked at George with narrowed eyes. "No way!" he exclaimed. "Why would that happen?"

"Don't doubt me," George urged. "This Medicare scheme is so lucrative and so easy, drug dealers and organized crime rings are getting into it. There's more money to be made with less risk, and if you do get caught, Medicare fraud carries shorter prison sentences than drug trafficking."

The hesitancy went out of the recruit's eye. "Remember that bank robber...what was his name?"

George grinned, knowing he'd scored. "You thinking about the bank robber, Willie Sutton?"

"Yeah. Didn't he say he robbed banks because that's where the money is?"

"You catch on fast!" George chuckled as the two men shook hands.

CHAPTER 16

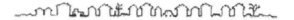

"WHAT IN THE world is she up to now?" whispered Laurie. "I swear, she's getting battier by the day!"

Laurie and Kim were peeking around the corner of the house, watching Mrs. Kingham as she searched the yard with a stick in her hand. Every so often, she'd stop, stoop, and stir something with the stick.

"Do you remember what day she started doing this?" Kim whispered back.

"Uh, I think it was a day after she was messing with the vacuum cleaner bag. But it would be crazy to think that had anything to do with what she's doing now."

"The rain kept us out of the back yard until today. Let's wait until she goes into the house and then try to remember where she was doing that thing with the stick."

Mrs. Kingham, intent on stirring, suddenly stopped, thrust both arms into the air, and yelled, "Yes!"

"Crazy woman! Now she's yelling to herself!" Kim whispered.

"Look! She's picking up something and talking to it!" Laurie sighed. "I wonder how long it would take me to learn how to read lips."

They watched as Mrs. Kingham threw the stick away and headed for the house.

"Well, she's gone, so let's play Detective!"

The girls found the first site with no problem; their noses led them to it.

"Poop! Mrs. Kingham was stirring Lucky's poop with the stick!"

"Go get the bags, Kim. We haven't picked up after Lucky since before the two days of rain. While he's here, that's our job, you know."

When Kim returned with bags, the two of them searched the yard. Every deposit they found had Mrs. Kingham's stick marks.

Inside her room, Mrs. Kingham looked out her window into the back yard. Initially shocked at seeing the girls searching for something, she calmed herself down when she remembered that they had the job of cleaning up after Lucky. That they were doing it now, right after she had inspected every one of the piles, was upsetting. But a closer look confirmed that picking them up was all they were doing. Anyhow, she'd found what she'd been looking for.

On the day that Molly had cleaned up the juice glass that Kim's flailing arm had sent flying along with Anita's ring, she had waited until no one was looking for her. Since the industrial vacuum was kept in the garage, she had managed to open the door quietly and slip out of the house. Once in the garage, removing the bag had been no problem. The fact that it was full made it hard to handle, but she had been confident she could split it open and find the ring.

What she hadn't done was look at the clock; if she had, she would have seen that it was dog-feeding time. Lucky was always fed at the same time each day, and here at the Hatches' he was fed in the garage.

Just as she had the knife poised to do surgery on the full vacuum bag, the access door had flown open, and noisy Laurie and Lucky had rushed into the garage. Laurie was teasing Lucky, holding his full bowl of food high in the air, making him beg for it.

Amid Laurie's laughter and Lucky's barking, the knife had pierced the bulging bag. Dust, particles of dirt and debris had exploded from the bag along with a shiny ring that had flown through the air and landed in the raised bowl.

Mrs. Kingham had watched in horror as Lucky emptied his food bowl.

––––––––––

FAMILY ACTIVITY KEPT Mrs. Kingham busy until after the dinner clean-up and the completion of the bedtime routine for the twins. Finally, her chores done for the day, she was free to retrieve the ring from its hiding place.

Holding the ring in her hand, she inspected it. Aunt Jenny's ring had survived its journey through Lucky's innards; there seemed to be nothing wrong with it that a good cleaning wouldn't take care of. Mrs. Kingham smiled to herself. As soon as she got it all nice and shiny again, she'd call Harold. If he was available, he could pick her up and take her away from this place. Tonight was not too soon.

Since the girls were watching television, Mrs. Kingham felt safe to use their bathroom. It wouldn't take her long to clean the ring and, if she needed a brush, she'd use one of the brat's toothbrushes. It didn't matter which brush she would choose, it made her happy to think that long after she was out of this house, one of the girls would be using a dirty brush.

She was still smiling to herself when the door burst open. She whirled around in surprise as Laurie, in the middle of yelling, "I get first dibs on the sh…!" reached out with a quick reflex and snatched the ring as it flew out of Mrs. Kingham's soapy hand.

Mrs. Kingham recovered quickly. "Nice catch, Laurie! I noticed that the ring was dirty, and I was just making it shiny for you."

The girls looked at Mrs. Kingham as if she had grown another head. The Mrs. Kingham who had been pinching them and making their lives miserable was doing something nice for them?

"Uh, I guess, uh, well, thank you, Mrs. Kingham, uh, but you really didn't have to do that! It's not like it's a real ring, or anything like that!"

"W-w-what isn't a real ring?" stammered Mrs. Kingham.

"This ring." Laurie announced. "No diamond could be as big as the one in this ring and be real. It's just a play ring."

Mrs. Kingham was having trouble breathing.

Kim looked at the ring in Laurie's hand. "What's all that brown stuff?" she asked.

Horrified, Mrs. Kingham saw that some of the dog feces was embedded in the ring's crevices. "That's…that's polish. Yes, I was using a brown polish. It just needs to be rinsed off. Here, give it to me…."

Laurie pulled her hand away. "No, I can do that, Mrs. Kingham. Now, could you please leave? Kim and I have to wash our hair and it has to dry before we can go to bed. Tomorrow is picture day at school!"

With much reluctance, Mrs. Kingham backed out of the bathroom, her eyes fixed on Anita's ring that was now in Kim's hand.

"Well, what was all that about?" Laurie wondered.

Kim didn't answer. She was too busy looking at the brown polish on the ring. Holding it up to her nose, she sniffed. "Laurie, this brown stuff isn't polish; it's poop!"

CHAPTER 17

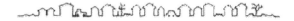

LOOKING RESTED AND relaxed, Joe entered the Omelet Shop and scanned the full room looking for Mitch. If Mrs. Kingham's cooking was as bad as Mitch claimed, Joe figured there was a good chance that Mitch would be breakfasting here.

Joe spied someone at a back table who was hidden behind a raised newspaper. On the chance that it was Mitch, he approached the table and cleared his throat.

As the person holding the paper slowly lowered it, Joe was surprised to see Molly's green eyes studying him.

"Good morning, Joe. Looking for anyone in particular?" she asked with a chuckle in her voice.

"Well, I wasn't really looking for you, but now that you're here, I just might have a cup of coffee with you."

"Pull out a chair, grab a cup, and help yourself; there's coffee in the carafe. You're looking particularly fit this fine morning!"

"Wait until you see Clara; she's absolutely radiant! Molly, I know we thanked you yesterday when we picked up Lucky, but let me say it again. The time Clara and I had together was wonderful! We never could have done it without you and Mrs. Haver."

"Keeping Lucky was a treat; we should thank you! Mrs. Haver must have been glad to see Jerry."

"Yes, she was, and Jerry was happy to see her. However, I think her feelings got a bit hurt because Jerry paid more attention to her dog Earl than he did to her. Kids!"

Joe poured himself a cup of coffee. "I don't often see you eating breakfast here. Now, with Mitch, that's a different story; he's here quite often, so I know all about Mrs. Kingham's cooking."

Molly nodded. "I really do have an early morning buyer, but don't think I wasn't happy to have an excuse to skip Mrs. Kingham's breakfast creation. When I left, the image of my family sitting at the table trying to pull their spoons out of a bowl of what was she claimed was oatmeal is burned into the retinas of my eyes."

Joe chuckled. "That's quite a picture!" In a more serious tone, he asked, "Are Laurie and Kim feeling any different toward Mrs. Kingham? Mitch thought there was something going on there."

Molly thought for a minute. "The girls have changed. We used to have such an open relationship! I don't know what's going on, but something is. I do believe they are spying on her."

Joe's eyes widened. "Spying? Could they be playing a game?"

"I suppose there are games that include spying, but I don't remember any game like that from my childhood days. Do you?"

"Well, we did play cops and robbers, and sometime that included spying on each other. But think of this; their uncle is a detective. Could they be playing some kind of detective game?"

"Did spying in your game of cops and robbers include pinching?"

"Now, you've got me. In this game, who is the pincher and who is the pinched?"

"Since both girls are sporting big black bruises and Mrs. Kingham isn't, I'd venture to say that Mrs. Kingham is the pincher."

Joe's mouth dropped open. "Are you sure that's where the bruises are coming from?"

"No, I'm not. Maybe the girls are playing rough games, but since they seem to be afraid of her, I just put the two things together…."

"And the girls aren't saying anything?"

"Not a peep. But you weren't looking for me this morning, were you? You were looking for Mitch. Does it have anything to do with the two men who came into my office?"

"You've got it," Joe nodded. "Clara went to a book signing yesterday. You know, the widow of the senator who died?"

Molly nodded. "And then she married the man who ended up in the ditch with our Anita." Molly paused to suppress a sob.

Joe waited for Molly to regain her composure.

"Yesterday, when Clara was in line to have her book signed, the writer looked up and waved at someone. Clara was surprised to see that the guy the author was waving at was the younger of the two men who stopped at your office the day Anita was murdered."

Molly was getting excited. "That's the one that Clara recognized when he was trying to lure Billy to his car with a piece of candy. Did Clara find out who that man is?"

"Yes, she did. When it was her turn to get her book signed, Emily Mills Fuller said the man she was waving at was Bernard Wing. Bernard's older brother is George Wing who owns some kind of medical company. She also added that her late husband, Mike, had worked for George before Mike's death."

"So, where does that leave us?"

"Right now? Nowhere. We thought that maybe they had stopped in some other real estate offices, but no other office reported seeing anyone who fits the descriptions of those two. Looks like they've left town."

LIFE WAS GOOD. Beginning to believe that hiring Mrs. Kingham had been the right thing to do, Molly sighed with relief as she left the restaurant and headed for her office. The search for Anita's replacement had been exhausting but fruitful. Granted, Laurie and Kim seem to have some issues with Anita's replacement, but Molly was positive that, given time, the two girls would come around. The bruised spots were troubling, but wouldn't the girls say something if Mrs. Kingham was hurting them?

Feeling carefree, Molly greeted her out-of-town buyers who were waiting for her in the office conference room. It was good being back at work. Finding the right house and matching it up with the right buyer was an art; over the years, Molly had perfected that art.

By the end of the morning, a tired buyer hugged Molly as she and her husband prepared to leave the office. "I can't believe how quickly you found the exact house for us! You turned what would have been a difficult transfer into something to look forward to."

Since they had already gone over the steps that the buyers had to take before closing on their new house, Molly smiled as she handed them the signed purchase agreement. "If you do all the things I've marked, I promise a smooth and trouble-free closing in a matter of weeks."

Clara was watching the satisfied look on Molly's face as the door closed on her buyers. "You look pleased with yourself!"

Molly stretched, poured a fresh cup of coffee, and sat down behind her desk. "Clara, I can't tell you how good it is to be back in action! I haven't felt this free to be here at the office since we lost Anita."

"Is that your way of saying that Mrs. Kingham is working out?"

"Oh, we've had our moments, but, yes, I think we hired the right woman."

Clara giggled. "I've been hearing stories about her cooking."

Molly nodded. "You got me there! Mrs. Kingham's cooking *is* pretty awful. However, some of the concoctions she comes up with are surprisingly tasty. Last night for dinner, she served chicken with something white on top of it. When I asked what it was, she just shrugged and said mayonnaise."

"It was good?"

"Very good. Breakfasts are imaginative, too. Jelly on the pancakes and syrup on the eggs looks like a big mistake, but I heard the girls requesting it the other morning."

"How is she with the twins?"

"Fine. When I get home from work they're always clean, their diapers have been changed, and they are usually asleep in the playpen."

"And the girls?"

Molly shrugged. "There seems to be a bit of a problem there. The girls actually appear to be afraid of Mrs. Kingham. I watch, but I never see her do anything that would make them fearful. Well, there is the matter of big black and blue marks on both the girls' arms…."

"What? You think she's hurting the girls?"

"Well, something is going on, but the girls haven't said a word. They do play some rough games, you know, but don't you think they'd tell us if Mrs. Kingham was hurting them?"

CHAPTER 18

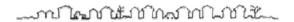

TAPPING HER FOOT in anticipation, Mrs. Kingham stood by the window overlooking the driveway. The girls had been invited to a birthday party, and since Molly had to work, she'd arranged for another mother to pick them up. Mrs. Kingham was looking forward to having free time to look for Anita's ring.

"Girls, your ride is here!" she called.

Laurie and Kim, each with a present under her arm, came running. Putting on her pleasant face to greet the mother, Mrs. Kingham opened the door. When Kim ran past her clutching a cat hand puppet, her favorite toy of the day, the pleasant look vanished. That Kim was taking her hand puppet to a party was not the problem; the sight that made Mrs. Kingham gasp was the necklace the cat was wearing. It was Anita's ring.

Mrs. Kingham's stammering and waving arms caught the attention of the mother. "Oh, don't worry about your charges!" she exclaimed as she rushed to open the car door. "I promise to take good care of your girls, and I'll bring them back after the party. It's wonderful that you're so concerned! I only wish I could be lucky enough to find someone like you!"

She stood in the doorway for a long time after the car had driven away. Horrified, she had watched Kim casually waving the hand puppet as she crawled into the car. What were the chances the cat would be wearing the necklace when Kim brought it home? Because of the huge diamond in the setting, the entire world thought the ring was just for play.

The crying twins finally got her attention, and with a big sigh, she turned and closed the door. To her, the sight of both babies, their mouths repulsively open and howling, was extremely irritating. The noise seemed to reverberate through the quiet house; a walk in the park would shut them up.

Mrs. Kingham pushed the double stroller into the park, found her favorite bench, and sat down. Sensing the lack of motion, both babies howled in protest. From experience, she knew that if she let them cry long enough, eventually they'd tire themselves and go to sleep.

With both babies fast asleep, Mrs. Kingham dozed off. It never entered her head to wonder why there was no one else in the park. If she had paid attention, she would have heard on the news, or read in the paper, that severe thunderstorms were predicted for today.

With her head resting on the back of the bench, the first raindrops hit her face. Jerking awake, she frantically looked around. Shocked at the rolling thunder, flashes of lightening, and pelting rain, she jumped to her feet, clutched her coat against the cold, and ran for home.

Feeling almost warm again, Mrs. Kingham crawled out of the bathtub and dried herself with a huge fluffy towel. She couldn't remember a time when she had been so cold. Just thinking about it, she rubbed the growing goose bumps off her arm.

Looking at a clock, she mentally started to plan the evening meal. She grinned as she thought of last night's dinner. Why she had smeared mayonnaise over the chicken before putting it in the oven was a mystery. The chicken had looked so bare, she'd grabbed the first thing her hand had encountered when she opened the refrigerator. What if she had grabbed the mustard jar? Chuckling to herself, she looked at the clock; time to feed the twins. Just the thought of feeding them the wretched-looking stuff that came out of the baby food jars made her wince. It was hard for her not to make a face while the babies eagerly ate the stuff. The twins…the twins… the twins…. Something jarred in her memory.

The park! She had left the babies at the park!

Frantically, she threw on some clothes, pulled on her sodden shoes, grabbed an umbrella, and ran out the door. Would the stroller still be there? What if someone had already found the babies? Moving faster than she had in years, in a matter of minutes she was within sight of the park. Through the pouring rain, she ran in the direction of her favorite bench, hoping upon hope that the stroller would still be there.

She heard the babies before she saw them.

The car bringing Laurie and Kim back from the party was filled with chatter and laughter. The party girl had been surprised, the ice cream and cake had been delicious, and the games had been fun. The mother who was driving the car was enjoying the happy chatter and therefore was unprepared for the sudden shout from the back seat.

"That's Mrs. Kingham pushing the twins! It's pouring rain! What is she doing out in this storm? I swear, that woman is nuts!"

"Oh my goodness! Should I stop?"

"Our house is just in the next block. By the looks of her, she can't get any wetter. I'm just worried about the babies."

"Do you have any idea why she would be walking in this storm? It's been raining like this for some time now!"

Kim had her mouth open to say something, but closed it when Laurie gave her a stern look and shook her head.

"We'll talk about it at home," she whispered to Kim.

THE BABIES HAD gotten very quiet. The only sounds Mrs. Kingham heard as she rushed toward home were the pelting rain hitting her umbrella, her own labored breath, and the squishing of her water-filled shoes. In her charge to get back to the house, she hadn't seen the passing car with the returning party-goers.

Alarmed at the changing color of the babies' faces, her brain whirled with ideas for her own survival. What if they died? Calling Harold was an option; she could be long gone before anyone discovered what she had done. On second thought, she decided that was a bad idea. Harold was good, but Detective Mitch Hatch was better. The thought of hiding for the rest of her life from the twins' revenge-seeking -detective father wasn't an appealing one. But wait! Maybe she didn't have to do anything more than just cover her tracks. With enough time, she could make this all go away. She'd get rid of the wet clothes by putting them into the dryer, and the babies' natural color would return after sitting in a tub of warm water. If the babies got sick, she could play innocent. All was not lost; she could do it! She almost smiled.

Her almost smile vanished when the car full of party-people pulled into the Hatches' driveway.

She had run out of time.

CHAPTER 19

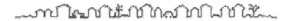

"TIME TO GO HOME!" Molly called out to Clara in the next room. "I sure did enjoy today."

Clara chuckled. "You had reason to enjoy your day. That was a big house you sold in a matter of a few hours."

"Hey, when you're good, things like that happen!" Molly replied with a laugh. "It wasn't just the big sale that made it such a good day; it's the peace of mind I have knowing that Mrs. Kingham has everything under control at home."

The phone rang.

LAURIE STOOD IN the front hall, praying Molly would soon rush through the door. Since neither of the girls had taken to Mrs. Kingham, Molly had questioned Laurie's whispered phone story. From upstairs, Laurie could hear water running into the tub and in the laundry room, the dryer was running. Mrs. Kingham was doing away with the evidence, and if she could make the twins lose that weird color, Molly wasn't going to believe Laurie's story. The twins were crying, but not with their usual robust resonance.

Kim walked slowly down the stairs and joined her sister. "Laurie, when Mrs. Kingham put the twins into the tub, she was talking to herself loud enough for me to hear what she was saying. It was as if she was giving instructions to someone about what to do about high-po-ther-me-a. Have you ever heard that word before?"

"No. What else did she say?"

"'Warm, not hot, warm, not hot'…that's what she kept muttering over and over. Do you have any idea how to spell that long word? We could look it up in the dictionary."

Before Laurie could respond, the front door flew open and Molly rushed in. "Where are they?"

The girls pointed.

Molly followed the strange sound of bleating lambs to the open door of the bathroom. The sight of her babies' red skin and barely open eyes shocked her. Mrs. Kingham, muttering "Warm, not hot", was frantically trying to keep both babies from falling over into the water.

"Mrs. Kingham! What on earth is going on?"

"Oh, it's you," the woman replied. "We got caught in the rain. The babes just need to be warmed up. No big deal."

"How long were they wet?"

"Not long. I ran home as fast as I could. I'm not as young as I used to be, though," she joked and faked a chuckle.

Molly picked up Tom and was surprised that even though he had been in warm water, his skin felt cold. Handing Mrs. Kingham a towel, she said, "Get Jill out, and let's find some warm clothes. I'll heat bottles for them, too."

The girls stayed in the background. "When are we going to tell Aunt Molly what we think happened?" Kim asked.

"She won't believe us. Maybe we should tell Uncle Mitch. After all, he's a detective. Detectives have to put pieces of the puzzle together all the time. Maybe he'll listen to us."

"Someone has to," Kim muttered.

Molly and Mitch spent the evening huddled around their babies who, by bedtime, looked almost normal. Their color was a healthy pink, their skin felt warm, and both were sound asleep.

"Wonder what really happened today?" Molly murmured to Mitch.

"What do you mean by that? Mrs. Kingham said they got caught in the rain. Is there more to the story?"

Molly sighed. "The girls seem to think so."

"Really? Like what?"

"There's something going on between the girls and Mrs. Kingham. I know they don't like her, but they won't say why."

Mitch shrugged. "Probably the whole thing has to do with her replacing Anita. They just haven't accepted that Mrs. Kingham is not Anita and never will be. They'll catch on. I'm not worried."

"That's a good theory, but we know Laurie and Kim are brighter than most kids their ages. I think we should pay more attention to them. I'd feel really bad if she was mistreating our girls and we hadn't picked up on it."

"Don't you think the girls would tell us if she was?"

"Well," questioned Molly, "have they told you about the black and blue marks on their arm? They sure haven't told me."

Their conversation was interrupted by a loud sneeze from the nursery.

Laurie and Kim hadn't had a chance to speak to either Aunt Molly or Uncle Mitch. It was bedtime and they had put themselves to bed; no kisses or stories tonight. Worry about the twins who were taking turns sneezing had occupied Molly and Mitch.

The girls were almost asleep when their door flew open, the light went on, and Mrs. Kingham entered. Shutting the door behind her, she whispered loudly, "Wake up!"

"Wha…" exclaimed Laurie.

"Just be quiet, you two. I have something to say."

Both girls, now wide-awake, sat up.

"I know you've been spying on me, and I know you've found out things that you want to tell your uncle."

The girls gasped.

"Just know this. *You* can tattle, but the babies can't. Any trouble you make for me, I'll pay you back by hurting them. You won't know what I'm doing to them, just know that they *will* be punished for your actions. *I mean what I say*!"

Mrs. Kingham gave them a motherly smile, shut off the light, and left the room.

"Oh, no!" wailed Kim.

"What's wrong?"

"I just wet the bed!"

CHAPTER 20

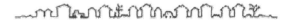

GEORGE WING WASN'T pleased. He had hoped that the man he had chosen to replace Mike would be fully trained by the time he and Bernard returned to the small western Michigan town. The man standing before him looked the part, but that's as far as it went. When it came to actual therapy, his new recruit was all thumbs.

"You still haven't gotten the hang of it, Harold."

"Have any of my patients complained about me?"

"All of them."

"All? That's kinda hard to believe."

"Believe it, Harold. I guess Mike spoiled me. He made it all look so easy…I sure miss that guy!"

"I'm tired of hearing about how great he was! All day long while I'm trying to learn this physical therapy crap, I hear Mike did this, and Mike did that…like he was some kind of a goddamn saint!"

George smiled. "Mike a saint? Now, that's a novel thought! No, Mike was not a saint, just a very likeable guy. I didn't think he had an enemy in the world, but I guess he did."

"Any headway on finding out who murdered him?"

"None. As far as I know, the authorities aren't even interested. It's as if he wasn't important enough for them to waste their time. The woman in the ditch with Mike got more attention than he did. I never could figure that out."

Harold sucked in a breath. There was no reason George needed to know that the woman in the ditch with Mike was Anita, Harold's sister.

"So, Harold, I'm giving you one more week to practice with a real physical therapist. It's not brain surgery, for heaven's sake! Learn the moves, learn the words…better yet, learn to spell the words!"

Harold hung his head. He'd dropped out of school to go into the family business with his mother. The required written reports that went along with the therapy were giving him sleepless nights. Not only was spelling the words a problem, pronouncing them was almost impossible.

"I'm doing a good job of getting the medical assistance identification numbers, aren't I?" he asked like a child needing a pat on the head.

"That part seems to come naturally to you, Harold. I guess it should, since that's what you and your mother have done for years. By the way, how is Agnes? She must be pretty old by now."

"Mom's doing fine. She's off on a little job, and knowing Mom, I'm sure she'll soon wrap it up!"

"You have every reason to be proud of her. That's one of the reasons why I'm expecting great things from you, Harold. You did very well in getting information from the people that you did see. We were able to use their names and numbers for additional expensive medical treatment. However, I'm giving you one more week to perfect the actual therapy part. Right now, you're a weak link in our chain. We can't afford to have our patients question our professionals."

The last time Harold remembered feeling like this was after a session in the principal's office. Unable to forget the less than enthusiastic remarks about his therapy ability, Harold repeatedly probed George's negative points much as a tongue worries a sore tooth. So engrossed was he in rehashing the conversation and inventing things he could have said if only he had thought of them, he almost missed seeing Bernard.

Harold knew that Bernard was George's younger brother, but that was as far as it went, except for several overheard conversations about him. The content of those remarks hadn't painted a pretty picture. Word was that George barred Bernard from the family business.

It was the furtive way Bernard had looked in all directions before hauling a bike off the rack that caught Harold's attention. Harold shrugged. It looked as if Bernard was up to something, but that wasn't his problem; Bernard was George's problem.

It was such a nice day, and since there was another bike on the rack just calling out to him, Harold convinced himself that a bike ride was just what he needed to salve his wounded pride. Even though he would have denied that he was following Bernard, he'd have a hard time explaining why he took great care not to be seen.

The easy ride that had started out on pavement quickly turned into a bumpy challenge on a two-track logging road. Veering off the weedy seldom-used trail, Harold almost missed seeing Bernard turn onto an over-grown path. Using the trees for cover, Harold watched as Bernard dropped his bike and disappeared into the woods. Propping his own bike against a tree, Harold looked around to make sure he'd be able to come back for it. With the location firmly in his mind, he plunged into the woods, taking what he hoped would be a shortcut to wherever Bernard was headed.

It was the sight of the beautiful red convertible, not pedaling the bike, that had sent Bernard's heart racing. There it was, just as he had left it the day he had murdered Mike.

When Mike had picked up Bernard to take him to Emily's book signing, he had been driving a newly leased car. The lease had expired on his old car, and in a spur-of-the-moment decision that morning, he had turned in his old black one and signed a short three-month lease on the convertible. Mike had chuckled when he told Bernard that he was looking forward to seeing the shocked look on Emily's face when she saw the car.

This was the first time Bernard had worked up enough courage to visit it. Initially, he had spent hours getting rid of fingerprints; now he felt sad, knowing that all he could ever do with the car was to admire it. No one had known that Mike had talked him into going to the book signing. Never had there been a hint that Bernard had anything to do with Mike's murder, and Bernard meant to keep it that way. The car was the only link. He wished that he hadn't called attention to himself as he had driven through town. But he had. Someone was bound to remember the red convertible and its exuberant driver.

The sound of movement in the woods caught his attention. An animal? He had recently seen a herd of deer in this area. Smiling with the anticipation of seeing the beautiful animals up close, he was startled when a man appeared at the edge of the clearing.

Harold had been aware that George had a brother, but Bernard knew nothing about Harold. To Bernard, the man who had discovered the car that would tie him to Mike's murder was someone involved in the investigation.

Bernard couldn't believe his luck, both good and bad. It was bad luck that an investigator had found Mike's car, but it was good luck that he was here to silence the man.

Bernard raised the gun, aimed, and fired.

Harold's shortcut had turned out to be a good one. As he was about to enter a clearing, he realized he had found Bernard quicker than he had anticipated. What he saw made no sense to him; Bernard, with a gun in his hand, was standing by a red convertible.

The expression on Harold's face before he pitched to the ground was one of utter confusion.

CHAPTER 21

"PLEASE, LAURIE," whispered Kim, "can I crawl in with you?"

"For heaven's sake! I can't believe you actually wet your bed."

"But I was scared! Weren't you?"

"Of course I was scared. Mrs. Kingham is evil!"

"Should we wake Molly?"

"I really don't want to. The twins finally quit crying so Molly is probably sleeping. It can't be that hard to change sheets…we've watched it being done zillions of times."

"Ah, come on! Just let me sleep with you. Please?"

"Ugh, you smell, Kim! You aren't getting into my bed! Go take a shower and change your pajamas."

"And then can I crawl in with you?"

"No. I'm gonna go look for clean sheets."

With soiled sheets and Kim's pajamas in the laundry hamper and clean sheets on the bed, two girls were quietly going back to sleep when Kim broke the silence.

"My hand puppet!" she cried, sitting up. "What happened to my hand puppet?"

"Oh, I meant to tell you. You peed on your hand puppet, too. I put it into the hamper to be washed."

"Ugh! Did you have to say it like that?"

"Well, you did."

Silence.

"Kim?"

"What?"

"Didn't the puppet have a necklace?"

"Yes, but it was just Anita's play ring."

"I didn't find the ring in your bed."

"That's because I left it at the party."

"Why would you do that?"

"Because Ruthie liked it. She promised to give it back."

"Oh, all right. Good night."

"Night? I think it's about morning," giggled Kim.

Mrs. Kingham unplugged her cell phone from the charger. If the twins got any sicker, and if the loaded silence coming from Mr. and Mrs. Hatch turned into actual accusations, she needed a working phone to call Harold. It was a relief to know that one call to her son would get her away from the screaming infants. Their colds had produced coughs, congestion, and aching ears. It took both the Hatches and Mrs. Kingham to get through the nights.

She knew she wasn't supposed to call Harold until she had the ring and was ready to be picked up, but the need to talk to him was impossible to ignore. She hit speed-dial and waited. He would yell at her, she knew, but it would be worth it just to hear his voice.

In a heavily wooded forest, a deer, startled by a sound coming from the trunk of a red convertible, disappeared into the trees.

———————

MOLLY HAD A puzzled look on her face as she slowly hung up the phone.

"Something wrong?" asked Mitch. The two of them were at the breakfast table, trying to muster the energy to face a new day. Neither one had gotten much sleep in the past few nights.

"You mean other than having sick babies and two girls who won't talk to us?"

"Yes, I already know that. But that phone call put funny little lines across your forehead. So what gives?"

Molly grinned and massaged her forehead. "That call was from Ruthie Vale's mother. Our girls went to Ruthie's birthday party the day of the big rain."

"Oh, no! Did our girls do something out of line?"

"No, nothing like that. She was calling about Anita's ring. You know, that really flashy one with the big fake diamond in it? Kim has been using that ring as a necklace on her hand puppet."

Mitch chuckled. "I noticed that. Quite a creative kid is our Kim!"

"Ruthie liked the ring, so Kim let her keep it for just a few days. Ruthie knew she had to give it back."

"So what's the big deal? Why the call?"

"Ruthie's granddad owns the jewelry shop here in town. He and his wife showed up after the party to give Ruthie her birthday gift. That's when he saw the ring. Mitch, that ring is not costume jewelry. That ring is for real!"

The sip of coffee Mitch had just taken turned into a stream as it spurted out of his mouth and across the table.

CHAPTER 22

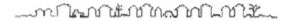

STANDING OUTSIDE GEORGE'S office, Bernard had watched the furious face of his brother as he yelled into the phone. He couldn't make out all of the words George was shouting, but the swear words were coming through loud and clear. It all had to do with Harold, the missing physical therapist. "What is it about this position?" George was yelling at the person on the other end. "First Mike, and now Harold."

When he was told it was Mike's replacement who was missing, it took all his acting ability to remain calm. There was real fear in Bernard's heart that George was planning to groom him for the vacant spot. The thought of having to place his hands on old decrepit and wrinkled bodies was enough to make Bernard physically ill.

The man that he had killed and stuffed into the trunk of the convertible wasn't an investigator after all. There were so many questions that had no answers. How had Harold gotten there, deep in the woods? He had searched the area for a car, but there was no car to be found. Obsessing over the matter was keeping him awake at night. However, being realistic, he knew that it didn't really matter who the man was or how he had gotten there; anyone finding the car had to disappear. If only he hadn't been such a show-off! He, who had never done anything violent in his life until recently, was starting to have trouble looking at himself. Shying away from mirrors, shaving had become a problem and most days the cowlick on the back of his head stood up straight. At night, his dreams were laced with bits and pieces of ditches and red cars. Dark circles under his eyes, and a nervous tic twitching his nose, grew more noticeable as the days passed.

He was eating when someone mentioned that a bike had gone missing from the rack. His hand shook so badly, the fork had trouble finding his mouth. Out there, somewhere along the logging road, Harold had left the bicycle. It had to be just a matter of time before the bike and the red convertible were found.

And then what?

———————

WITH A BABY across her shoulder, Mrs. Kingham leaned her exhausted body against the wall. Jill, one of the twins, screamed in protest as she pulled on her own already angry-looking red ear. With a big sigh, Mrs. Kingham pushed herself off the wall and continued the walk through the dark house. Tommy had finally cried himself to sleep. Both Molly and Mitch were in bed, and here she was, still walking. If she wanted to be fair, she would have to admit that she was the reason the twins were ill. However, in her present state, thinking clearly wasn't even possible.

The ring had never come back from the party. From snatches of conversation Mrs. Kingham had learned that, after the value of the ring had been discovered, the ring had been placed in a safety-deposit box. Since there was no chance of her ever seeing the ring again, her mission was over. It was time to call Harold and disappear, but there was a problem with that; Harold wasn't answering his phone. Was he back in jail? He had promised her he would stay out of trouble until she had the ring in her possession. Thoughts of what she would do to her son when he eventually came to get her out of this hellhole propelled her legs to move and move…ah, Jill was finally asleep.

CHAPTER 23

MOLLY CHUCKLED AS she got out of her car and waved to Clara, who had just pulled into the office parking lot. The sight of Lucky riding through town on his miniature fire truck had generated smiles and, once again, business for Allen Real Estate.

"Good morning, Clara, and good morning to you, Lucky!"

"Well, I didn't expect to see you, Molly. Are the twins over their colds?"

Molly shook her head. "No, but I just had to get out of the house. I can't stay here very long because Mrs. Kingham is acting funny and the girls aren't talking to me."

"Ouch! Doesn't sound like it's sunshine and roses in the Hatch household!" Clara remarked as she bent down to unbuckle Lucky's harness. "Cut that out!" she yelled as Lucky, his tongue out, was preparing to give her a sloppy kiss.

Neither one spoke as they made their way into the office, switched on lights, and turned on the coffee maker.

"Molly, this Mrs. Kingham…could she be the reason why the girls aren't talking?"

"I don't even want to think about it! We looked so long and so hard to even find someone like Mrs. Kingham…I'd hate to have to start all over again. Anyhow, her story when she came to us was that she had been living with her daughter and taking care of her grandkids when the daughter remarried. The new husband didn't like Mrs. Kingham and made her leave. According to her, if we didn't hire her, she would have to go back to the assisted living home where she was presently renting a room."

"So you're stuck with her? What are you going to do when she gets too old to be of any help to you? Set her up in a little apartment in your attic?"

"Oh, Clara," laughed Molly. "You and your imagination!" She lowered her coffee cup. "What I'm not imagining is the change in the girls. I found soiled bed sheets in the clothes hamper this morning. I tried not to be judgmental and make one of them feel guilty, but neither of them is talking."

"Oh, my goodness! One of them is *really* upset! Any more bruised spots on their arms?"

"No new ones…at least I haven't seen any."

"Are they doing anything else?"

"You mean other than hovering over the twins like guardian angels and watching Mrs. Kingham's every move?"

"They're doing that?"

"Yes, and the girls don't want to go to school. They're pretending to be sick; they fake coughs and sneezes, and they invent teacher's planning days so they can stay home."

"But they won't talk to you. Hmmm…sounds as if Mrs. Kingham is holding something over their heads."

"That's what I'm afraid of. If that's the case, we would *really* have to get rid of the woman." Molly sighed.

Since neither one could come up with a solution to the problem, both silently sipped their coffee.

Molly's face brightened; she had just remembered the ring.

"Oh, Clara! Do I have a story to tell you!"

———

WITH A PUZZLED look on her face, Mrs. Kingham's rush into the nursery came to an abrupt halt. A vague feeling that there was something *really* important that she needed to do was nagging her, but try as she might, she couldn't remember what it was.

Unprepared for the weight of the two girls who slammed into her, she staggered into the wall. Regaining her balance, she glared down and hissed, "So, following me again, eh? You think I haven't noticed? Well think again. I raised two evil boys who tried to pull every trick in the book on me. I know them all!"

Before the girls could declare their innocence, the smoke alarm in the kitchen sounded. Mrs. Kingham slapped her forehead. "That's what I was trying to remember! I left something on the stove!"

The sight of flames shooting into the air from the content of a skillet left on the burner caused Mrs. Kingham to clutch her chest and freeze.

"Do something!" yelled Kim.

No sound was coming out of Mrs. Kingham's moving mouth.

"Mrs. Kingham! Do something!" Kim screamed. "You're supposed to be taking care of us!"

Shaking herself out of her trance, she ran to the sink and grabbed a glass. "Water! We need water to put out the fire!"

"No!" shrieked Laurie as she knocked the glass out of Mrs. Kingham's hand. The glass shattered.

"Now look what you've done! I'm not taking the blame for that!"

"I just saw a movie about this in school last week! Get out of my way, Mrs. Kingham!" cried Laurie. "Kim, be careful, but I want you to turn off the burner!"

Grabbing a dishcloth, Laurie wet it, wrung it out, and then as she cautiously approached the flaming pan, she threw the cloth over it.

The fire fizzled, and then went out.

The alarm was still blaring when the door opened and Molly rushed in.

It was bedtime at the Hatch household; the absence of babies crying was unsettling.

"Do you hear what I hear?" whispered Mitch.

"What are you talking about? I don't hear anything!"

"That's what I mean," Mitch replied. "How long has it been since our house has been this silent?"

"Hmmm. Since before the day of the big rain," Molly whispered back.

"Tell me again about the kitchen fire. Do you realize we could have lost the house and everyone in it, if Laurie hadn't known what to do?"

"I get goose bumps just thinking about it. By the way, I called Laurie's teacher to thank her for showing that movie to the class. According to Miss Watson, if Mrs. Kingham had thrown water on that pan…."

Mitch pulled Molly close and hugged her.

Molly was just drifting off to sleep when Mitch spoke quietly. "I was just thinking…remember the day of the big rain? You said something strange that day; I've been thinking about it."

With a big sigh, Molly rolled over. "Now you're accusing me of saying strange things? What did I say?"

"While we were listening to Mrs. Kingham's account of the story, you had a funny look on your face, kinda like you didn't believe her. In fact, you made a remark that I haven't forgotten."

"I did?"

"Yes, you did. 'I wonder what really happened' is what you said."

"I did?"

"So I asked you if there was more to the story than just Mrs. Kingham and the twins getting caught in the rain."

"I really don't remember any of this. What did I say?"

"You said, and here I'm quoting you, 'Laurie and Kim seem to think so'."

Molly sat up, sleep forgotten. "Yes, I remember now!" she exclaimed in a wide-awake voice. "The girls were acting as if they had something important to tell me, but they never had a chance; we were both involved with warming the babies. Mitch, if I'm not mistaken, that was the last time the girls talked to us about anything!"

"Dare we think that the girls know something about Mrs. Kingham, and she's threatening to do something to them if they tell us?"

"Or threatening to do something to the twins," Molly added quietly.

With a quick intake of breath, Mitch demanded, "What makes you say that?"

"You aren't around enough during the day to watch those girls. They're never far from the babies. The other day when I was telling Clara about it, I called them guardian angels."

"You were talking to Clara about our problems?"

"Come on, Mitch! Clara is like family. Anyhow, after one of the girls wet the bed…"

Now it was Mitch's turn to sit up in bed. "What did you say?"

"I found soiled sheets in the laundry hamper the other morning. Neither girl is talking. Clara has the opinion that the black and blue marks on the girls' arms and the bed wetting have to do with their being afraid of Mrs. Kingham."

"Why am I just hearing about this?" Mitch demanded loudly.

"Calm down, and lower your voice," Molly hissed. "I'm enjoying our quiet house."

"Sorry about that!"

"I didn't tell you, because whichever girl did it, I'm sure she's embarrassed. It would be the last thing she'd want her Uncle Mitch to know. But if it happened again, I planned on telling you."

"After hearing all of this, I'm feeling very uncomfortable. We both have jobs, the girls go to school, and that leaves our babies home alone with Mrs. Kingham."

"Mitch," Molly's voice trembled. "What have we gotten ourselves into? What if Mrs. Kingham isn't the perfect live-in help we thought we were hiring?"

"Something's not quite right. Her story about her daughter's new husband kicking her out was true; Heather was living in an assisted living facility when she applied for this job."

"Well, until we figure this out, I'm not leaving my babies alone with her. I'll take them to the office with me if I have to."

Silence.

"Mitch, did you go to sleep?"

"No, I'm just thinking. How can we get the girls to talk to us? We had such an open relationship before all this happened. How do we get that back?"

"Let's sleep on it. I'm so tired right now it's hard to think straight."

"You're right. But I do know that tomorrow I'm going to contact the assisted living facility and ask some questions."

He was answered by a muffled snore.

CHAPTER 24

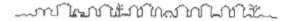

MITCH HELD THE silent telephone in his clutched fist. How did this happen? And how was he going to explain it to Molly?

Heather Kingham was dead. She had died in the town's assisted living facility shortly before a woman by that name had answered their advertisement for a live-in position. This information had come, not from the facility itself, but from one of the residents who had been Heather's friend.

According to the authorities Mitch had alerted, the proprietor had not reported her death. Her social security checks were still arriving at the home, along with payment to the owner for her expensive drugs and therapy sessions.

Who was living in their house? Where had she come from, and why was she there?

"OH, HI, MITCH!" Molly said as she tucked the phone under her chin; it took both hands to handle the diapering task. "What's up?"

"Have the girls left for school?"

"No, but they're about to. Why do you ask?"

"I'm on my way home right now. Keep the girls with you, have the twins ready, and I'll pick all of you up in fifteen."

"Wha…?"

Mitch had hung up.

In the flurry of securing all passengers, there was no chance to talk or ask questions. The grim look on Mitch's face was causing Molly's stomach to knot. As they pulled into the parking lot of Allen Real Estate, she asked, "I suppose you're going to tell me why we have just arrived at my place of business?"

"Clara is expecting us. We're leaving the twins with her."

"With Clara? Are you sure she agreed to do this?"

"Yes, she did."

"And, pray tell, what are the rest of us going to do?"

"We, my dear, are going out to breakfast!" announced Mitch.

"The Pancake House, The Pancake House!" shouted Kim.

"Yes, The Pancake House it is!" The grim look on Mitch's face dissolved into a smile. "We're going to have a good old family breakfast together!"

As stomachs were filled with syrupy pancakes, eggs, and bacon, the mood around the table was warm and comfortable. The girls had dropped their defenses and were laughing about the things Lucky had done while in their care. When Kim started to tell about the poopy ring, Laurie shushed her. "That's not something to talk about when we're eating."

Mitch held up his hand. "There's no subject we can't discuss at this table. In fact, that's why we're here. Many things have happened and we need to talk about them."

Laurie stole a look at Kim, and shook her head.

"Laurie, I saw that!" Mitch exclaimed. "Now is the time to tell all. I promise, nothing bad is going to happen to you."

Kim burst into tears; Laurie's eyes shot daggers at her sister.

Mitch cleared his throat. With a little information, he was counting on changing the girl's determination not to talk.

"I have some things to tell all of you. What I have to say is shocking and unbelievable. I don't know all the answers; I'm counting on the rest of you to share anything that might shed light on the subject."

Forks were dropped and mouths stopped chewing; he had their attention.

"Mrs. Kingham is not who she says she is. As of now, we have no idea why she claims to be Mrs. Kingham. The real one is dead."

Mitch waited for the chatter to quiet down.

"What we do know is Heather Kingham's best friend in the assisted living home was a woman by the name of Agnes Foreman. Agnes has a son, Harold, who visited her. However, Agnes disappeared directly after the death of Heather Kingham. Working past all their assumed names, my investigators dug deep and came upon a very disturbing fact. The mother-son team has been quite successful in many fraud cases that are still open."

Mitch stopped talking, took a drink of water, and then continued. "Agnes Foreman gave birth to three children. We're only concerned with two of them; one was Harold that I've already mentioned, and one was a daughter Agnes named…Anita." The last word in his sentence was spoken so low, the three at the table couldn't believe what they had just heard…or thought they'd heard.

"Did you say Anita? As in *our* Anita?" whispered Molly.

Mitch couldn't speak; he just nodded.

"Anita's mother is living with us?"

"Looks that way."

"Oh, come on now…that doesn't make sense! Why wouldn't she tell us she was Anita's mother?"

"I've no idea." Mitch looked around the table at his little family. "Do you remember that Anita told us she was an only child and that her parents were dead?"

Molly made a face. "Well, I guess if I had a mother and a brother like Agnes and Harold, I might try to pass myself off as having no family, too. Remember, no relative came to her funeral."

The girls were listening intently, their eyes following Mitch and Molly as they talked.

Molly squirmed. "This is making me feel very uncomfortable. Do we have any idea why this woman named Agnes answered our ad for live-in help?"

In a small voice, Kim offered, "We know why she came to live with us."

Molly looked at Kim in astonishment. "You know? Did she tell you?"

Both girls shook their heads.

"So how do you know?"

"Because we watched her," giggled Laurie. "She was looking for something."

Kim laughed. "I got up on Laurie's shoulders and peeked through the windows. I watched her dump all of Anita's things on the floor."

Molly thought back to her conversation with Tom; the girls had been spying!

"Did she find anything?" asked Mitch.

"No, and she got so mad, she just jammed the stuff back into the drawers and slammed them shut."

No one talked for a bit, and then Laurie continued with the story. "Remember the day when Kim flung her arm and sent the juice glass flying? Well, she had the ring that Anita gave us to play with on her thumb, and it flew off and landed in the smashed glass. I was about to grab it when Mrs. Kingham pushed me aside and reached for it. That's when you, Molly, came in with the industrial vacuum and cleaned it all up. I guess you sucked up the ring, too, because I never saw it until…"

Kim yelled, "It's my turn. I get to tell about the poopy ring!"

The story was good for a laugh, but when things quieted down, Molly asked, "How did the ring get out of the vacuum bag and into Lucky's stomach?"

Mitch raised his eyebrows. "I think I know. I found a big mess in the garage that involved a slashed vacuum bag; dirt, dust, and dog hair was scattered over a big area. Laurie, didn't you feed Lucky in the garage while he was with us?"

"Yes, I did. And one day Mrs. Kingham was in there doing something with a knife. What do you think happened?"

"If the bag was full enough, I can see something like a ring exploding out of it and landing in Lucky's dish. That's the only explanation I can come up with as to how the ring got into his stomach."

"So after she found the ring in Lucky's droppings, how did you get it back?"

Laurie finished the story of how she had caught the ring after it had slipped out of Mrs. Kingham's soapy fingers.

"What are you thinking now?" Molly asked Mitch. "Do you think that very valuable ring is what Mrs. Ki…Agnes was looking for? Is that why she pretended to be someone she wasn't, just to live with us and look for it?"

"Very likely. With the size of the diamond and the price of gold today, that ring is worth a little less than half a million. But aside from the fascinating ring story, I'm more interested in the day of the big rain. Girls, I think you know something about that day, and Agnes is threatening you if you tell."

Molly looked at Mitch. "Should we be calling her Agnes now instead of Mrs. Kingham? Are you that sure of your information?"

Mitch shrugged. "Let's just hear the rest of the story before we worry about what to call her. So, girls, what was the threat?"

The girls hung their heads. "She was going to hurt the babies," Kim whispered. Laurie nodded.

Molly choked. "She threatened to hurt the twins?"

"Yes, she said we could tattle, but the babies couldn't, so if we told you anything, she'd take it out on them."

Molly's face turned white.

Mitch reached out and took their hands. "You don't have to be afraid any more. That woman won't be around to hurt anyone. She's history, so girls, please tell us what you know."

The girls looked at each other, and then relaxed. Maybe it was all right to tell.

"Well, to begin with, she talks to herself all the time. We had fun trying to read her lips, but we never got good enough to figure out what she was muttering about," Kim stated.

"Yeah," Laurie said, "And she forgets where she is, and what she should be doing. But one day she forgot the twins at the park and started to walk home without them. Kim and I watched her turn around and go back for them. They weren't in any danger because we were still there…she'd forgotten about us, too."

"Those black and blue marks," Molly asked, "did she do that?"

"Yes, she claimed we sassed her. I never knew what she was talking about, but she pinched us anyway."

Molly cringed.

"Tell us about the rainy day," Mitch urged.

"That was the day of the birthday party. The storm had been going on for some time, and it was still raining hard when we drove by her and the twins. She was about a block away from the house when we passed her. We think she took the twins to the park before it started to rain, then forgot about them and ran home when the storm started. Something probably made her remember, and she went back and got them."

Remembering how cold her babies had been when she'd taken them from the bathtub, Molly shuddered.

Laurie continued. "If we hadn't come home so soon, she probably could have gotten away with it. She knew we had figured it out, and that's when she threatened to hurt the babies if we tattled on her."

All conversation stopped when the waitress presented the bill.

Molly looked at her husband. "I think we've heard enough. Let's face it; we were so desperate for help, we took one look at the grandmotherly woman and figured she was the answer to our prayers. I'm just grateful nothing really bad and irreparable happened to our children and our home. Now it's time we head back to my office and relieve Clara from her stint with the twins; she's not used to taking care of infants. How did you ever talk her into doing it in the first place?"

"With an offer she couldn't refuse!" Mitch was smirking, and his eyebrows were dancing.

"And that would be…?"

"A second honeymoon, her choice of when and for how long, and we get the three boys, plus Lucky, for the entire time."

Molly's jaw dropped. "You've got to be kidding!"

Mitch grinned. "Yes, I'm kidding, but I sure did get a reaction out of you!"

The Pancake House staff got their chuckle for the day when they watched a small redheaded woman cuff a laughing man on the back of the head.

CHAPTER 25

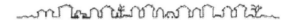

SNEAKING A PEEK through the motel window that overlooked the parking lot, Bernard watched George climb out of his car. When the early morning alarm had gone off, he pretended he hadn't heard it. Feigning sleep, he waited until George had showered, dressed, and left. He didn't know where his brother was going, and he really didn't care. His biggest worry was that one of these days George was going to take a good look at him.

Keeping secrets from George was the problem. Now that Bernard had three murders to hide, he lived in constant fear that his big brother was going to become aware of the change in his appearance. George was so busy adding layers of participants to his medical fraud network that he had yet to notice that Bernard's clothes no longer fit, that his eyes were blacked-rimmed, and his nose twitched.

Ignoring the fact that George had emphatically forbidden him to use his car, he grabbed the extra set of keys. As George made his way to their room, Bernard ran out the back door of the motel and into the car. Driving aimlessly through town, he not only wished that he had somewhere to go, he also wished that he had someone to go there with him. Bernard had no friends. Oh, there was Jimmy, George's errand boy, but he wasn't really a friend; he was an employee. What he needed was a *best* friend, someone who he could trust. The weight of what was simmering inside him was becoming unbearable. Each day brought him closer to the exploding point. Just thinking about it now, in the quiet of the car, his breathing quickened, his heart raced, and his palms grew wet. The reality that he had murdered, yes, *murdered,* three people was flowering into a full-blown panic attack. His fingers clutched the steering wheel as his vision blurred.

The approaching intersection with its dangling red light went unnoticed.

———————

AGNES FOREMAN KNEW when to hold and when to fold; over the years, her skill at playing cards had served her well.

Life in the Hatch household had become edgy. The weighted silences, the conversations that ceased when she walked into the room, and the fact that Mrs. Hatch had taken over caring for the twins told her that it was time for her to get out. She had failed in her mission; the ring was gone. At first, she was scared to tell Harold, but as time went on and Harold wasn't answering his phone, she would have been happy just to hear his yelling voice.

It was time to fold.

She had known something was amiss this morning when Mr. Hatch returned home, loaded the entire family in his car, and drove away. The silence of the empty house shouted at her. Packing her one bag didn't take long, and with a final slam of the front door, she headed toward town. Her plan was to get away from the house before she called a taxi. Strange, but going back to the hated assisted living home didn't sound so bad. Harold had said her room was paid for, and she was sure that when he surfaced, that's where he'd go to look for her.

Deep in thought as she approached a busy intersection, she took it as a good omen that the green light was flashing the inviting word 'walk'.

So, that's what she did. Swinging her one bag, she walked.

———————

119

BLINDED BY THE panic attack and unaware of his surroundings, Bernard drove into the intersection

The thump of the impact and the sound of something landing on the roof of the car jarred Bernard out of his stupor. Slamming on the brakes, he skidded to a stop. The road was still empty of cars; whatever he had done, no one had seen it. Safe inside the car, his eyes scanned the area, curious about what he had hit. A deer, perhaps? A big dog? Knowing that a wounded animal can be dangerous, he cautiously opened the door, ready to jump back in if he needed to.

He never saw it coming; an arm slid off the roof of his car and struck him on the head. Whirling around, he came face to face with an elderly woman whose unblinking gray eyes stared at him. He screamed, stopped to take a breath, and then he screamed again.

By now, the light had turned green. Hearing the grinding gears of an approaching truck brought him back to reality. Dragging the lifeless body off the roof, he staggered under its weight as he opened the back door and shoved her in. He jumped behind the wheel and sped off as the truck entered the intersection, tailgating him until he picked up enough speed to put distance between them.

It was late afternoon by the time Bernard returned to the motel parking lot. Looking up at the window, he saw George's angry face peering down at him. Bernard fixed a fake smile and steeled himself for what was to come. One thing George couldn't fault him on was the condition of the car. It actually looked better now than when he had driven off with it this morning. Since the damage to the car had been minimal, the marks of the impact had been easily rubbed out. His best hope was that George would be so pissed about his missing car that he wouldn't notice that the clothes Bernard had on were new. Cleaning up the car after he had transferred the woman's body to the trunk of

Mike's convertible had wrecked his old ones. At least, his new clothes fit.

Deep in the woods off a remote logging road, a mother bear and her male offspring sniffed around the trunk of a car that now held a human mother and *her* male offspring.

CHAPTER 26

THE TRIP HOME from The Pancake House was a quiet one. Clara had met them at the office door with a finger over her lips, claiming she had sung the twins to sleep. Molly, who had heard Clara's version of what she called singing, figured they had gone to sleep in self-defense.

Molly and Mitch rode in silence, each one thinking how they were going to confront Mrs. Ki...Agnes. Both were having trouble accepting the connection between Agnes and their much-loved Anita.

Scared because they had tattled, the girls also rode in silence. Mitch and Molly weren't always going to be around to protect them. Should they have kept their mouths shut?

When the car came to a stop in the driveway, no one made a move to get out. Mitch cleared his throat. "Let's try to be quiet and not wake the babies. What we have to do now is going to be hard enough without adding their crying to the mess." He turned and faced the back seat; the two girls were hugging each other.

"She's gonna hurt us!" whimpered Kim. "You don't know her like we do. She never pinched you!"

"Yeah," added Laurie. "She was always smiley and nice around you two."

Ashamed, Mitch hung his head. He was a detective who should have spotted a deception that could have harmed his family. "Girls, I'm so sorry we brought that woman into our home. But she's history; she won't be around to hurt anyone. Now, it's time to get out of the car and into the house. Might as well get this over with."

Mitch was surprised to find the door to the house unlocked. "Molly, I was the last one out of the house this morning, and I'm sure I locked the door behind me."

"Well, it's not locked now, so get out of my way. I want to get the twins settled before they wake up."

Leaving Mitch behind in the entrance pondering over the unlocked door, the girls ran through the house. He was still standing there when he heard them yelling.

"Hey, you two, you're going to wake the babies. Knock it off!"

"But…" Laurie called.

"No buts about it, be quiet!"

Molly appeared at the top of the steps. "Mitch, I think Mrs. Ki…Agnes is gone!"

"That's what we've been yelling about," panted Kim.

"Gone?" Mitch repeated. "Gone?"

"We just checked her closet. It's empty and so are all the drawers," Laurie called down from the top of the stairs.

Mitch shook his head. "I didn't see this coming, but I should have. According to my investigators, that woman has been in con games all her life. Picking up negative reactions from us the past few days probably tipped her off."

"She can't be gone!" wailed Molly. "Who's going to answer all my questions?"

Mitch looked at Molly's distressed face. "You wanted to ask her about Anita, didn't you?" he asked quietly.

"I loved Anita! I can't believe our wonderful Anita came from such a mother! And what was the name of her brother?"

"His name is Harold. Believe me, Agnes has quite a rap sheet, and so does her son."

Molly slowly descended the steps. "Where could she have gone?"

"Probably to Harold. Maybe he even came here and picked her up. If the girls are right and she was here to find Anita's ring, then there was no reason for her to stay once she knew it was in a safety deposit box."

Molly thought for a bit, and then she said, "Well, I'll probably never know the answers to my questions, so I'll just be glad that she's gone. You're right; she's probably with Harold."

FOR THE THIRD time in so many days, Bernard stood at the edge of the clearing and gazed at the red convertible. Like a magnet, the two bodies in the trunk kept pulling him to this spot. The dead man had to be Harold, Mike's replacement, but who was the woman? There hadn't been any mention of a missing elderly woman either in the papers or on the news. Since she was clean and well dressed, why wasn't someone missing her? Dead gray eyes staring at him stole his sanity and his sleep. Who was she?

As he turned to leave, a rustling noise from the woods on the far side of the car caught his attention. A glimpse of something brown didn't alarm him; probably just a deer from the herd he had seen the other day.

Bernard was not the only one gazing at the red convertible. Mother bear, who had staked out the good smelling contents of the trunk, was concerned. She was waiting to see if the creature, who was between her and her cub, was going to enter the clearing.

CHAPTER 27

THE FAILURE OF an assisted living home to report the death of one of its occupants was reported to the Medicare contractor system. However, with one set of contractors paying claims and another combing through those claims in an effort to stop billions a year in fraud, the report fell through the cracks. George Wing, the new owner of the home, breathed a sigh of relief.

Now that his business was no longer being investigated by Medicare, he had the time to relax and think of other things. Pouring a fresh cup of coffee, he looked out the window in time to see Bernard riding past on a bicycle. Something about his brother didn't look right. Was he combing his hair differently? Had he lost weight? Before he could come to some conclusion, the phone rang.

The sight of his brother standing at the window looking at him was enough to send searing shots of fear through Bernard's body. The thought of being caught, and he knew that he would be, was crippling his ability to think. After searching the Internet and learning that Michigan had done away with the death penalty in 1847, he was briefly relieved. However, he was thrown back into a panic when the insight hit; he would spend the rest of his life behind bars. Staring into the impending doom that would be his future, he added vomiting to his growing list of afflictions.

Now, riding blindly away from the questioning look on George's face, Bernard wasn't even surprised when he found himself on the two-track road, heading for the convertible. On one of his trips, he had stumbled upon Harold's bike. Unable to handle two bikes, he had simply rolled the bike further into woods where it had disappeared into an overgrown plot of poison ivy. What were the chances that someone would venture into such a patch and trip over a bike? He wished the convertible were so easily concealed. Instead, it stood in the clearing, shining in all its glory, waiting for someone to discover it. The odor coming from the trunk was another matter. Just standing at the edge of the clearing, he could smell it. He had noticed that the number of animal tracks increased as the days went by. Sometimes, when he approached the clearing very quietly, he could hear the scurry of fleeing feet.

Swallowing back the bile that was rising in his throat, he straddled the bike and headed home.

––––––––––

THE CRIMINAL INVESTIGATORS in the Fraud division of the FBI had been alerted of an unreported death in an assisted living home owned by George Wing. The new owner of the home pleaded innocent, blaming the confusion caused by the change of ownership. Investigating that went deeper into the home's history failed to produce any other incident. The FBI crossed George Wing's name off the list of possible fraud participants.

The U.S. Marshal sat at his desk, his hand on the phone, debating with himself; should he share what had been told to him, or should he forget about it? The information had come quite accidentally from someone in the witness protection program, a man who was a resident of the home recently sold to George Wing.

As in any job, some people are hard to forget. The man who had taken the name of Mike Fuller when he had gone into the witness protection program was one of those people. Someone had murdered Mike. The protective service has an unblemished record; no witness who followed instruction had ever met foul play. Unfortunately, Mike had not followed orders. Against strong objections from the U.S. Marshal, Mike had wormed his way into the suspected medical fraud network headed by George Wing.

His mind made up, the marshal picked up the telephone and called the fraud division of the FBI. They needed to know that Mike Fuller, a protected witness, had been murdered while in the employment of George Wing.

IT WAS CLOSE to noon when Clara glanced up as the office door opened. The sight of a disheveled and agitated Molly brought her to her feet. "Whoa, girl! You look like something the cat dragged in!"

"You don't know the half of it!" Molly muttered through clenched teeth as she pushed the double stroller into the room.

"Did you give Mrs. Kingham the day off? Is that why you brought the twins to work with you?"

"Ha, don't I wish! There is no Mrs. Kingham, or to put it another way, there never was a Mrs. Kingham."

"Are we into riddles now?"

Molly called over her shoulder as she pushed the stroller into her office, "Give me a minute to get the babies settled then, if you'll bring me a cup of coffee, I'll entertain you with an unbelievable tale!"

The story that had unfolded during breakfast at The Pancake House was told over howls. Both women walked, each soothing a teething baby on their shoulder; they passed each other as they circled the desk.

"So, Agnes Foreman was Anita's mother," mused Clara. "I'm having a problem wrapping my brain around that picture."

"I had so many questions I wanted to ask about Anita, I couldn't wait to get home from the restaurant. Now, I'll never know."

"Well, it would have been a nasty scene if she had been there when you got home."

"I know. I know it's best that it happened the way it did. I can't help wondering where she went, though."

"Probably with that no-good son of hers. I predict that when you find one, you'll find the other."

CHAPTER 28

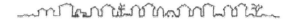

TED FOREMAN STEPPED away from the curb and watched the bus that had brought him from prison to this little western Michigan town pull back into traffic. It had happened; he was out, he was free. Turning his head toward the sky, the warmth of the sun on his face brought tears to his eyes. His whole body quivered with anticipation; he'd been dreaming for years about this day.

Not wanting Harold to see his tears, he quickly wiped them and looked around. Harold had been very definite in his instructions. Ted looked at his watch; he was right on time. Where was Harold? Maybe something came up at work with that George person. With luck, maybe George would give him a job.

He wasn't looking for his mother, because Harold had told him that she was working a con, trying to get back Aunt Jennie's ring. Once they had the ring, they'd be fixed financially. He didn't remember his Aunt Jennie, his mother's sister, but, according to the family tales, Jennie was a beauty who had caught the eye of a Chicago gangster. Until the day he was shot down in the street by a rival gang, he had showered Jennie with gifts. Before her death, Jennie had given one of those gifts to Anita, the only member of the family who had a conscience. Now that Anita was dead, the ring belonged to the rest of the family. He had no doubt that his mom would pull off the con. After all, hadn't she been the one who had schooled both him and Harold in the fine art of cons and frauds?

Where was Harold?

A stranger standing on the street corner in a small town was fuel for curiosity; he was getting some serious stares. Looking around, hoping to find a place to sit while he waited for Harold to show up, his stomach growled, fueled by the smell of bacon and eggs coming from the Omelet Shop on the corner. He had been too excited to eat breakfast, his last meal in prison, before boarding the bus. He'd give Harold another half hour, and then he'd head for the restaurant. After that, if Harold was still a no-show, he had another idea. Being the good sister that she had been, Anita had corresponded with him over the years. He knew the name of the family where she had worked; that's where Mom would be.

DETECTIVE MITCH AND Fire Chief Joe were finishing their late breakfast when the door of the Omelet Shop opened and a stranger walked in.

"Did you see that?" whispered Joe.

"See what?" Mitch whispered back. "And why are we whispering?"

"That guy that just walked in? Wanna make a bet with me?"

"Depends on the odds. What's the bet?"

"Just know that if I win the bet, you'll take Lucky for a long weekend."

"You and Clara planning another honeymoon? How many do you think you guys are entitled to?"

"As many as we want. Now here's the bet. That guy that just came in? I'm betting he just got off the prison bus."

"And I'm to bet that he didn't? What makes you think that he did?"

"Oh, his clothes, his pallor, and his scared look when he saw my uniform."

"Someone scared of a fire chief's uniform? You wish!"

"The bet, Mitch, the bet."

"Hmmm. I have to think on that for a minute. But as far as taking Lucky for a long weekend, it's not worth a bet. The girls would love it because as it is now, they're being neglected. Molly and I spend all our time caring for the twins."

"Are the bags under her eyes as big as the bags under yours?" teased Joe.

Mitch sighed. "I'm afraid so. Do babies ever sleep through the night?"

"Let's get back to the subject."

"I'm not betting one way or another."

"You're no fun! But I was serious about your taking Lucky for a long weekend."

"Just tell us when, and drop him off. But I think you'd win the bet if we'd made one. See the way that guy is huddled over his food? Kinda like he's protecting it. I think you're right."

"Okay, here's another bet."

"Man, you're full of it today! So, what's the new bet?"

"I'll bet we see that guy again."

"Hmmm," replied Mitch.

CHAPTER 29

Thunk!

Bernard, his head bent over the toilet, sobbed in resignation. Reaching up, he pushed the toilet seat back in place. Vomiting was humbling enough without adding the indignity of getting hit on the head by the falling seat. He checked his sobs when a sharp knock on the bathroom door was followed by George's anxious voice. "Bernard, are you all right?"

Oh, shit. "Yeah, I'm gonna be okay. Must've been something I ate. Go back to bed." He held his breath while George remained outside the door. "Go on, George. I'm fine!"

Hearing George walk away, Bernard slid to the floor. He was in hell. Most of his days were spent trying to stay out of George's sight. Now that George had heard him vomiting, he could only imagine the grilling he would get at tomorrow's breakfast table. He needed to get away. But how? He had no money. George wasn't stingy about giving him money when he asked for it, but always having to tell him why he needed the money was humiliating.

Following George around to the different assisted living and nursing homes was making him physically ill. This, added to the consuming remorse that he had murdered four people, had turned him into the walking dead.

His sleepless nights were filled with elaborate and unworkable moneymaking schemes. He had no talents, nothing to offer the world in exchange for money to flee his nightmare life. Exhausted from pacing the floor, he finally flopped down on the bed. Just as the blissful feeling of impending sleep settled through his body, the answer to his problem came to him. He did have something of value to sell; he had information.

Sleep forgotten, he turned on his computer and connected to the Internet. He remembered reading an article about a whistleblower receiving a huge payoff for squealing on his employer. Bernard's fingers flew over the keys, bringing up articles on the False Claims Act.

If the Justice Department wins the case with information given to them by the whistleblower, the whistleblower is entitled to a maximum of 25% of any recovered money.

Bernard sat back and reread the statement. Could he do it? Could he rat on his brother? Where and how could he survive until he received the payoff? Searching his memory of the article, he typed *Witness Protective Agency.*

Going from one site to another, he learned that the program would create a new identity for him and place him in a city where he most likely wouldn't be recognized. That sounded good to Bernard. If no one knew his new name or where he was, how could they pin the four dead people on him? Another site informed him that housing, subsistence for basic living expenses, medical care, job training, and employment assistance would be provided. As far as choosing a new name, he could have his pick. However, it was suggested that he keep his current initials or the same first name. The court would do the name change like any other change, but the records would be sealed.

They'd help him find a job? Since Bernard had never held a job in his entire life, he really didn't like the sound of that. According to the cases he'd read about, even whistleblowers that presented evidence much less than what he could provide, had been rewarded millions of dollars. What if his case wasn't settled for years? Did that mean he'd be all alone in some strange city, working at some menial paying job until he came into his millions?

Dawn had lighted the sky on a new day, but he hadn't noticed. Reading quickly, he was overwhelmed at the steps involved in becoming a whistleblower. First, he had to go to a state or federal law enforcement agency and submit a request for protection. Did that mean the state police? The application would then be submitted to the OEO. The OEO? Who in hell was the OEO? The OEO would then go to the Marshal's Service. If the Marshal Service agreed, its recommendation would go back to the OEO.

After visiting more sites, he found that OEO stands for Office of Enforcement Operation, the agency that authorizes or denies the entry of all applicants into the federal Witness Security.

He was leaning back in his chair, congratulating himself on making progress, when he smelled coffee. For the first time in weeks, he felt hungry. The task of becoming a whistleblower was truly daunting, but just the glimmer of hope that he might get out of the mess he had made of his life was a relief. A big relief.

TED FOREMAN RAN his fingers over the pages of the telephone book. He remembered that Anita had told him she was working for a family named Hatch. That's where his mom would be, working as live-in help until she found the ring. There were two such names in the book: Richard Hatch and Mitchell Hatch.

Checking Richard's address, he drove to the street and parked for several hours. Anita had also told him that she had been hired to take care of infant twins, so when he saw an elderly man pushing a garbage can to the curb, Ted reasoned he had the wrong house. He chuckled to himself, imagining his mom taking care of babies. She was never shy about expressing her feelings about infants; she had never liked her own, and certainly not other people's babies.

Mitchell's house was a different story. Two young girls, playing with a huge dog, ran in and out of the house, a small haggard-looking redheaded woman pushed a double stroller into the park, and a tall, blond man appeared on the patio and worked on the grill. This had to be the right house, but where was Mom? Shouldn't she be the one pushing the babies?

Unaware that they were being watched, Laurie and Kim chased Lucky, who was theirs for the weekend, around the backyard. Not really understanding the game, Lucky stopped, flopped to the ground and rolled over, inviting the girls to scratch his belly. The resulting pile-up of bodies produced screams of laughter, cover for the noise Ted made as he scrambled from his hiding place into the security of the garage. He had watched Hatch leave the house, the girls were playing with a dog, and the redhead was back pushing two howling babies up and down the sidewalk. Did that mean Mom was inside the house?

The door into the house wasn't locked. Ted spent no time in the family living area; he headed upstairs to where his mom's room would be. He quickly found the master bedroom and the girls' room. Mom had to be in the one last bedroom, the one with the closed door. Was she ill? That would explain why the redhead was pushing the stroller.

Gently knocking on the door, he whispered, "Mom, it's me, Ted! Open up!"

When he heard nothing but silence, he knocked again. "Come on, Mom! Let me in before someone sees me. Open up!"

He gave her a few seconds to reply before he turned the knob and stepped into an empty room. A quick look into the bare closet told the story; Mom wasn't living here.

Hearing voices approaching the house, he ran downstairs and out the back door without being seen.

He needed to find Mom. Could he possibly remember the assisted living home Harold had put Mom in after the last blotched con? Since Harold seemed to be off the grid and Anita was dead, Mom was the only one left to contact. Knowing her, Ted was sure she would have the whole story.

CHAPTER 30

THE DAY HE asked George for permission to drive his car, Bernard couldn't look his brother in the eye. He was using George's car to drive into town where he would take the first step in becoming a whistleblower. If George had looked into Bernard's coat pocket, he would have seen papers with long lists of homes and columns of medical professional names. Bernard knew that the more fraud he reported, the greater would be his reward.

Two young men who were looking for a place to ditch their mother were chauffeuring George today; those were their words, not George's. His only request was that Bernard return the car to the assisted living home.

No matter how hard he struggled, Ted couldn't come up with the name of the home where Harold had stashed their mother. How many homes like that would be in a town this size? The telephone book listed just one.

Driving his rental car slowly through the town, he easily located the home. One lone parking spot right in front of the building caught his eye. Preparing to park, he was caught off-guard when a car pulled in front of him and stole the parking space.

Ted was fuming when a short young man dressed in clothes several sizes too large for him stepped out of the car and flashed him the finger. Instant rage propelled Ted out of his car.

Bernard was feeling good about himself. The first meeting had gone smoothly; the casual feel of the gathering disappeared when Bernard handed them the papers with the list of homes and participating professionals. Now his job was to act normal around his brother until he had completed all the steps and disappeared into the witness protection program with enough reward money to live high on the hog for the rest of his life.

Parking around the home was a problem this time of the day. Ahead he could see only one empty space, and he intended it to be his. Never stopping when he noticed that another car was preparing to park there, he pulled around it and slid into the spot. Today was his day. High on the success of his first step in getting out of this miserable life, he stepped out and gave the finger to the driver of the car he had cut off.

The car door flew open, and charging at him with both fists raised was Harold, the same Harold he had killed and stuffed into the trunk of the red convertible.

Barnard's whole world had turned black even before his head hit the cement.

Ted, confused, stood over the man lying motionless on the road. He hadn't touched the guy, and yet it was obvious that he was out cold. He was in the process of nudging him with the toe of his shoe when a shout came from the house. "Harold! Where the hell have you been? You've got a lot of explaining to do!"

Ted cringed. It had happened again. Since he and his brother looked alike, they had spent their childhood being called by each other's names. Their time together as a family stopped in their early teens when they took turns spending time behind bars.

Ted watched the man run out of the assisted living home and down to where the body was stretched out on the road. Shocked at the sight, he yelled, "Harold, what did you do to my brother?"

Ted's brain was whirling. Harold had written Ted that he was working at the home for a man named George who had a younger brother named Bernard. So, this must be George, and Bernard must be the one lying on the road. Evidently, Harold hadn't been around for some time because George seemed really angry. Why not pretend to be Harold? He needed a job, and Harold was already working for this man.

"Hi, George!" he bluffed. "What's wrong with Bernard?"

"What do you mean, what's wrong? You hit him, didn't you?"

Ted shook his head. "Didn't touch him."

"You're telling me he just ended up on the road all by himself? Don't think so."

Ted shrugged. "Think what you want, George. That's what happened. He got out of his car and fell flat on his face. Go figure."

George looked down at his brother, his eyes taking in the slim body, dressed in an outfit that was many sizes too large. "Bernard hasn't been himself lately. Guess I haven't been paying enough attention to my brother. Think I should call an ambulance?"

"He hasn't moved a muscle since he fell."

George sighed, pulled out his cell phone, and dialed 911.

Bernard sat up and wildly looked around him. Where was he and how did he get here? Noticing that the people rushing around had on white coats with stethoscopes hanging out of their pockets, reality hit. Groaning, he lay back down and covered his face with his arm. The last thing he remembered was seeing Harold coming toward him with his fists raised. Reasoning told him that it couldn't be Harold, but his eyes told him that it was Harold.

Looking out in the waiting area, he could see George and Harold deep in conversation. Were they talking about him? Was Harold telling George how Bernard had shot him and stuffed him into a car's trunk?

That couldn't be! He had seen a dead Harold when he crammed the old woman into the trunk. It had been so crowded, he'd had to rearrange Harold's legs to get the lid to close. So who was George talking to?

George looked in at Bernard, and seeing that he had moved, motioned for Ted to follow. They walked to the bed where Bernard was lying looking up at the ceiling. "Bernard, can you hear me?"

Bernard nodded.

George had a catch in his voice as he talked softly to his brother. "Bernard, I'm *so* sorry. I was working too hard and I didn't pay enough attention to you. That's going to change." He swallowed a sob. "On her deathbed, I promised Mom that I would look after you, and I haven't been doing that."

Bernard rolled his head to the side and looked up his brother. George had tears in his eyes; he cared. Waves of regret washed over him. This was his brother, the only family he had left, and he had betrayed him. The result of his whistle blowing would put George behind bars for the rest of his life.

When the man who was calling himself Harold looked down at him and winked, it pushed him over the edge.

Bernard passed out.

CHAPTER 31

ONE OF THE jobs Ted had in prison was working in the hospital unit as a janitor. While collecting waste from the treatment rooms, he sometimes pretended to be busy, but actually, he was watching. The knowledge he had picked up from observing the professionals helped him in continuing the Harold charade.

George seemed to be pleased. "Harold, I'm glad to see that you took my criticism seriously. I know you didn't like it when I came down on you pretty hard because you stormed out of here and stayed away for weeks. I'm not even going to ask where you went...I'm just happy your therapy techniques are so much better."

So Harold got angry and split? Where did he go? And why does Bernard shy away from me? Since I've found that winking at him gets such a reaction, I'll do it every chance I get.

Ted hadn't figured out what shady deals were going on in the home. All Harold had told him in his letters was that he was pretending to be a physical therapist. Since Harold had never worked a straight job in his life, Ted was pretty sure some kind of a con was being pulled, but until George dropped some hints, Ted was in the dark. What he didn't like was working with the old coots in the homes and he had no plans to stick around. He wanted the ring; the ring meant financial independence. But first, he had to get his hands on it. Since both his sister and his mother had worked for the Hatch family, that's where the ring had to be. The thought that his mother had found the ring and she and Harold split, gave Ted some sleepless nights. But if Harold had been planning to skip with their mother, why had he contacted Ted in prison?

Not wanting to go back to that urine-smelling home, Ted took his time walking back to his car. He pulled the list out of his pocket and checked to make sure he had bought all the things George had written down. He didn't even know he was hungry until he walked past the Omelet shop. Remembering the good meal he had eaten in that restaurant the day he had gotten off the prison bus, he made a quick decision. The sign said 'Seat yourself', so he did.

He was studying the menu the waitress had placed on the table when he heard female chatter coming from the booth directly behind him. Listening, he quickly lost interest in the mother-daughter prattle until the word "Hatch" caught his attention. Wasn't that the name of the family both Anita and his mom had worked for? He quit reading and listened.

A mature female voice asked, "Ruthie, do you know what they did with it?"

"You mean after they found out how much money it was worth?"

"Yes. They aren't keeping the ring in their house, are they? Oh, my, I hope not! Your grandfather claimed it was worth almost half a million. I'd never sleep a wink if that ring was under my roof!"

Ruthie giggled. "I can't believe we used it to play dress-up. But, no, the ring is safe in some bank's box."

"Do you know what they're going to do with it?"

"They don't know."

"That's really not their ring. It belongs to Anita's family."

"Remember I told you that Mrs. Kingham, the woman they hired to take Anita's place, wasn't really Mrs. Kingham? The real Mrs. Kingham is dead."

"That was the wildest story you'd ever told me, and at first I didn't believe you."

"Motherrrrr!" wailed Ruth.

"But Mrs. Hatch called me, and it's true. The elderly woman who called herself Mrs. Kingham was really Agnes Foreman, the mother of their much loved Anita. They think she was there to look for the ring."

"Both Laurie and Kim were scared of that lady. She pinched them and said she'd hurt the twins if they told on her."

"What a mess!" exclaimed the mother. "Do they know where the woman went?"

"She was gone when the Hatches learned the truth and went home to confront her. Nobody has seen her since that day. I know Mrs. Hatch was sad that she never had a chance to ask the woman questions about Anita. How had she turned out so good when her mother was so awful?"

"She's probably with Harold then," the mother said.

"Harold? Who's Harold?"

"That's Agnes' son. Mrs. Hatch told me about him. It seems that Agnes and Harold worked scams together. I would imagine they'll eventually come back for the ring. It's their ring, after all. Are you going to finish your milkshake?"

"No, I'm too full."

"Well, then let's go. We still have to find you a pair of school shoes."

He heard the rustling of coats and packages as the booth emptied.

Well, wasn't that interesting! He lingered over his lunch, reviewing all that he had just heard: One, his mother had been calling herself Mrs. Kingham, for what reason he didn't know, and two, although Harold and his mother were together, they didn't have the ring because it was in a safe-deposit box in a bank, and three, the mother in the booth was right; that ring did belong to Anita's family.

What was the chance that he could get his hands on the ring and disappear before the other two members of the family showed up?

Ted left the restaurant with a half-formed plan in his mind. Why hadn't Harold and his mother just knocked on Mitch Hatch's door and explained that Anita had a very expensive heirloom that belonged to the family? That would have been too simple. Instead, from what he heard of the conversation in the restaurant, Mom had taken on the identity of a dead woman. Why had they made getting the ring back so complicated? Probably one of Harold's bright ideas.

Ted looked at his watch. George had loaned him his car for the trip into town for supplies; he was already late in getting back to the home. The thought of those old crones with their liver spots and toothless gums gave him the willies.

George's loony brother was another story. Ted was curious about Bernard's reaction toward him. Harold must have been holding something horrendous over Bernard's head because of the response he could get out of the man with just a wink. When that got old, Ted tried more things. He knew something was *really* wrong the day he had caught Bernard's eye and, with a smug look on his face, nodded his head.

Bernard had vomited.

All this was puzzling for Ted. George had accepted him as Harold from the very beginning, but not Bernard. In fact, Bernard had passed out the very first time he had seen him. How long could he keep up this pretense? He had a job, a place to live that included meals, and a car to drive when George didn't need it. Eventually, George would let it slip what con he was running, because Ted was certain he was. However, since Harold was already in on the details, George felt no need to talk about them.

Whatever it was, George was raking in money like a bandit. A fleeting thought bothered him. He needed to find out what George was up to, because if the business went south, he'd wind up in jail along with the rest of them. Going back to prison was something he never intended to do.

CHAPTER 32

"JUST WHO DO you think you'll be running into this weekend? An old boyfriend, perhaps?" teased Molly.

"I don't know how I ever let Joe talk me into going to my high school reunion. I didn't like it when I was there, so why should I go back now and relive misery?" Clara made a face. "I was so fat...."

"How fat were you?" chuckled Molly.

"Well, you know the Goodyear blimp? That fat."

Molly looked at Clara with skeptical eyes. "You weren't that fat when you came to work for me."

"That's because I had put myself on a liquid diet. For weeks, I ate nothing. When you saw me, I had just fallen off that diet."

"The liquid diet worked?"

"Yes, but as soon as I started eating again, the pounds came back with a vengeance. And having a tall, slim sister didn't help my morale a bit."

"Ha, I'll bet Marie isn't so slim now! How far along in her pregnancy is she?"

"Pretty far. But you'd never guess it to look at her."

"When you're as tall as Marie, there's plenty of space to grow a baby!"

"That's a funny way to put it! Want to talk about you? How did you find space for two in your five foot body?"

"You're forgetting about the half inch!"

"Molly, I've watched you get measured. You gain that half inch by standing on your tip-toes!"

"Whoops! You caught me," Molly laughed. "You certainly are slim now. Do you give Lucky all the credit?"

"That dog! Walking him back and forth from home to the office because he refused to get into a car started the big change. The breakup with Joe just before we got married got rid of the rest of it."

The room got quiet as the women remembered the weeks that Joe and Clara had been estranged. Clara had said some words that she regretted saying as soon as they had left her mouth; unfortunately, Joe had heard them.

Molly cleared her throat. "So, go to your reunion with your slimness and let them admire what you have become! Anyhow, how many of them were voted Realtor of the Year three years in a row? Answer me that!"

"That was Lucky's doings! He captured the evil Santa, he brought down Sammy the Grunt, and he did tricks at my wedding. I just was there to sell houses to the people who wanted to work with the owner of such a dog. How can I take credit for that?"

"It started because you didn't turn him away when he scratched at the office door. Most people would have, you know. So who's taking care of the home front while you're gone for the weekend? And by the way, since the reunion is here in town, why are you staying in the hotel?"

Clara sighed. "That's another one of Joe's bright ideas. There are many activities planned that extend into the late hours, so Joe insisted I stay at the hotel rather than drive home every night. Kinda like a mini-vacation, he says."

"And the boys?"

"The boys are going to Mrs. Haver again. She hasn't taken on any more foster children since Jerry."

"Is there a reason she hasn't?"

"She claims Jerry broke her heart when he left. In time, she says, she'll do it again, but now evidently isn't the time."

"And Lucky? Where will he go?"

"Joe will just take him to work with him."

"Why not leave him with us? The girls love to have him around. They've been begging for a dog of their own, but the way things are right now at home, there's no way we could add a dog. Mitch and I don't have much time to spend with the girls, and I feel badly about that."

"I suppose we could do that. I know Lucky likes the girls."

"Well, plan on any weekend. Just call before Joe drops him off at our house. Tell me about the dress you bought for the reunion!"

"I'd rather show you. It's with the seamstress right now being shortened. When I pick it up, I'll bring it back to the office and model it for you."

"Great! Oh, that's Lucky scratching at the door."

The huge dog entered the office and walked straight to his bed in the corner.

"You're staying longer and longer with Joe at the fire station these days," Clara teased. "Makes me think you love him more than you love me."

Soft snoring sounds soon filled the office. "You asleep already?" she asked the big dog who opened one eye, looked at her, and then closed it. "Is Joe working you too hard?"

The ringing phone stopped her one-sided conversation with the dog.

"Hello, Allen Real Estate"

"It's me, your loving husband. What's up?"

"You called me, remember?"

"Oh, that's right. I'm bored. Talk to me."

"Things slow there, too? I have Molly to talk to, and I tried having a conversation with Lucky, but he fell asleep in the middle of it."

"Well, at least you have him. He hasn't visited me all week. I'm beginning to think he loves you more than he loves me!"

"What do you mean he hasn't visited you? He just got back about five minutes ago. He's been gone all afternoon."

"You've got to be kidding! He sure wasn't here at the fire station."

"Joe, are you serious? He hasn't been at the fire station all week?"

"Why would I kid you about that? But if he wasn't here, then where was he? Do you think our dog has a secret life?"

"Well, if he has a secret life, it has to be a very active one because our dog is sleeping like a log. He's worn out!"

Joe laughed. "Do you think we should get Detective Hatch to look into this? Maybe he could follow Lucky and see where he spending his afternoons."

"Oh, before I forget, Molly asked if the girls could have Lucky the weekend I'm gone for the reunion."

"Wonderful! I just hope on this visit Lucky doesn't swallow a half million dollar ring!"

THE OEO AGENT watched Bernard as he paced in the waiting area. He'd seen other occasions when a person offering evidence to prosecute a wrongdoer had had a change of heart, but he never had had a whistleblower who was informing on a brother while still living under his brother's roof. By the looks of his loose fitting clothes, the man must have dropped twenty pounds. A facial tic, darting eyes and shaky hands were signs that he wasn't going to last until all the evidence was collected.

Bernard had to be removed from his brother's home. It was time to put him into the witness protection program.

They had talked about the program many times, but Bernard was still shocked when he was informed that the time had come for him to disappear; he was in danger. In danger? Did they really think his brother would harm him?

"Disappear? You're talking about right now? I have things to do, I have…."

"Bernard, we've discussed this many times. Would it help if we told you about another whistleblower? The one that that your brother eliminated?"

He whirled around, a shocked look on his face. "Eliminated as in kill? I don't believe you! My brother couldn't kill anything! I've seen him carry a bug out of the house and let it go. If he couldn't even kill a bug, how could he kill a person? Answer me that!"

"He doesn't kill anyone; he contracts someone else to do it."

Bernard looked in disbelief at the Marshall.

"Believe us, Bernard, it's true."

Bernard sighed. "How much time do I have?"

"Tomorrow. We'll send a car for you when you call and tell us the coast is clear. We want you to be home alone when we come for you."

CHAPTER 33

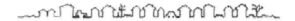

EMILY MILLS FULLER, the widow of Mike Fuller, stared at the paper she had just removed from an envelope with the name of a finance company on the return address. It informed Mike Fuller that the short-term lease he had taken out on a brand-new red convertible was about to end. Did Mr. Fuller intend to renew the lease?

Emily caught her breath and backed into a chair. Lately, she was remembering things that the shock of Mike's murder had buried. The memory of the last conversation she'd had with Mike was bubbling to the surface. It was…it was something about a…surprise! Yes, that was it! He was going to have a surprise for her when he picked her up to take her to the book signing. Could the surprise have been the red convertible? Now she was remembering something else. Didn't he say he was bringing someone with him to the signing? The police had been looking for Mike's car, but if Mike had traded his old one for the convertible, they'd been looking for the wrong car. And if Mike was bringing someone to the signing, where was that person when Mike was murdered?

Since the local police had seemed more interested in finding Mike's killer than any other agencies, she searched in her desk for a business card. There it was, the card that Detective Mitch Hatch had given her. She hadn't been impressed with Detective Miller, the one who had been assigned to the case.

As she picked up the phone to dial the detective, she remembered. Bernard. Yes, he was bringing Bernard to the book signing, and then

Mike had said something funny that had made her laugh. What was it? Her forehead wrinkled, and her eyes squinted. Ah, yes, it was something about Jesus. What could he have said about Jesus that was funny?

Mitch was having fun just watching the girls play with the huge dog. It was good to see the girls laughing. Life in the Hatch household since they had lost their live-in help had been full of tension. Molly had given up trying to go to work. That meant Clara, once again, was manning the office singlehandedly. Sleepless nights and busy days were taking a toll on both Mitch and Molly. Tempers were short, and words were said that should have remained unsaid.

Molly appeared behind the screened door. "It's good to hear happy sounds for a change," she said to Mitch, who was standing on the porch, watching the girls.

"Clara and Joe think we're doing them a favor by keeping Lucky over long weekends; in reality, they're doing us a favor. We've been neglecting the girls, and I don't know what to do about it. I feel bad that I have to turn them down when they ask for a dog of their own."

"Oh, please, Mitch! Keep nipping that request in the bud! The last thing we need is a puppy to housetrain."

Mitch grinned. "I did better than that. I told them the only dog I'd allow them to have was a dog like Lucky."

"What are the chances that there's another dog in the world that looks like Lucky?" Molly chuckled. "He's a mixture of generations of mutts."

"Let's forget about the dog issue and start thinking about finding another live-in. You know that we're going to have to start all over again."

"I get tired just thinking about all the women we interviewed before we found Mrs. Ki...Agnes. We thought that the gods were smiling down on us when we took just one glance at the grandmotherly-looking woman." Molly shook her head. "We made a bad decision, and I've lost all confidence in being able to pick a reliable live-in."

"We've got to do something, though. I get some sleep when the twins finally quiet down, but you don't. I can hear you walking around at night. Can't Dr. Parker come up with some kind of combination of drugs for your restless legs?"

"He's trying." Molly replied with a catch in her voice. "How can something that sounds so unthreatening cause so much torment? You don't die from restless legs, although some nights I've thought about cutting them off."

"Did you read that they've changed the name?"

"Changed the name? Why did they think they had to do that?"

"I suppose it's because just saying the name Restless Leg Syndrome is sure to get a laugh on the late night shows."

Molly shook her head. "So now what do they call it? The Twitchy Leg Syndrome? The Jerky Appendage Syndrome? The Suffering Lower Extremities Syndrome? The…"

"The new name is Willis-Ekbom Disease."

"You're joking!"

"No, I'm not. Go look it up."

"It's not a syndrome anymore? Now I have a disease?"

"Well, that's the change they've made."

"Do you think I should wear a mask over my mouth? Don't diseases spread germs?" Molly threw up her hands in defeat. "All I can say is, would a rose by any other name smell any different? I don't care what they're calling it now! My legs are restless at night, and it has nothing to do with either Willis or Ekbom." Molly was almost sputtering she was so upset. "They should have talked to me before they changed the name."

"Mrs. Hatch, why don't you tell me exactly how you feel?"

"I think I just did," Molly chuckled. "Oh, I hear the phone ringing. I'll get it."

Mitch was watching the girls chase Lucky around the yard when he heard Molly calling from inside.

"Mitch, it's for you."

"Thanks," he called as he reluctantly left the happy scene and walked back into the house.

"Hello?"

"Detective Hatch, I'm Emily Fuller, the wife of Mike Fuller…the man in the dit…"

"I know who you are, Mrs. Fuller. How can I help you?"

Molly watched her husband's face change as he listened. Whoever the caller was, Mitch was hearing something that had his full attention.

Officer Tom Allen and Detective Mitch Hatch arrived at the car dealership at the same time.

"This could be big!" Tom remarked to Mitch. "If the car Mike leased has one of those homing devices on it, it can be located."

"Cross your fingers. We haven't had one break in this case."

The manager of the dealership arrived and shook their hands. Because he was hearing the request from the proper authorities, he looked up Mike's leasing record and assured them that the car that Mike had leased did indeed have that feature.

CHAPTER 34

BERNARD WAS FIDGETY. Just the thought of getting away from the nightmare situation was both scary and liberating. One glance from George, and Bernard fell under the black blanket of remorse; one sideways glance from the man pretending to be Harold sent him into fits of fear. It would be good to get away from both of them.

He had made the call, his bag was packed, and he was ready to go as soon as a car arrived for him. The house was empty; both the fake Harold and George were off inspecting a new facility.

He stopped his pacing when a thought brought a wave of intense fear. What if the man pretending to be Harold was really Harold? What if he had only imagined that Harold was in the trunk when he had stuffed the old woman in it? What if….

Blind panic chased Bernard out of the house. Before he fell off the face of the earth and disappeared into a new identity, he needed to know. Not knowing was nightmare material for the rest of his life.

Pulling his bike off the rack, he headed for the two-track road deep in the forest. The bike seemed to have a mind of its own; that was fortunate, because Bernard was past being able to navigate. Turning off the rutted road, he headed in the direction of the clearing.

There it was. Standing in bright sunlight, shiny and beautiful, was Mike's convertible. He stood and stared. Did he have the nerve to walk to the car and open the trunk? What if he opened the trunk and Harold wasn't in there? Goosebumps covered his body.

On shaky legs, he slowly entered the clearing. His attention was focused; as he walked toward the car, he heard nothing, and he saw nothing. The smell was overpowering, but he didn't notice that either. As if in a trance, he reached out a hand and released the latch. The trunk lid slowly rose all on its own.

Feeling hot breath on the back of his neck, the fleeting thought flashed through his head that Harold truly was alive and had followed him here. To do what? Kill him and put him in the trunk? Maybe he could try to bargain, maybe he could....powerful furry arms came out of nowhere, wrapped around Bernard and squeezed the air from his lungs. His terrified brain tried to make sense out of what was happening as he felt himself being lifted off his feet.

The male cub watched as his mother hauled a struggling creature into the trees. The creature soon found his voice, scaring the cub with his strange sounds.

The cub was glad when the frightening noises stopped.

DEEP IN THE woods, Officer Tom Allen led a group of policemen from where their cars were parked on the two-track logging road. Detective Mitch caught up with them.

"Something ahead is dead," he remarked in a low voice. "Really dead."

"Yeah," Tom answered. "That's one smell that never changes. Makes me wonder what we're going to find."

"Hopefully, answers to lots of questions."

All conversation stopped at the edge of the clearing. A spotlight of sunshine shone down through the trees and bathed a red convertible in light.

"Well, would you look at that!" Tom murmured.

AND SO IT GOES

"It's right where the homing device said it would be. Wonder why the trunk lid is up?"

Tom gagged. "Did anyone think to bring masks?"

Shaking heads confirmed that no one had brought masks. With an arm covering his nose, each man made his way toward the car.

"Bear tracks!" yelled one of the cops. "They're all over the place!"

The men stopped. Indeed, there was plenty of evidence that large animals had been in the area; huge piles of scat dotted the clearing.

"Watch where you step, guys!" chuckled Mitch. "But you can relax. No bear is going to challenge a group this size unless we get between a mother and her cub. Just don't wander off."

Mitch's chuckle turned into a strangled sound when they got to the trunk; Agnes Foreman, her dead gray eyes open, stared into his. Stifling a yell, he stepped back, slamming into Tom who was standing behind him.

"God, Mitch!" yelled Tom as he recovered his balance. "That's your live-in help. How the hell did she end up here?"

Mitch was having trouble keeping his lunch down. Bending over, he staggered to the side of the group, trying not to breathe too deeply because of the stench. He could hear the chatter going on in the group.

"Who's the guy?"

"I've never seen him around town."

From the side, Mitch managed to find his voice. "The last time I saw those two together, it was on their rap sheet. That man is Agnes' son, Harold." He paused to swallow the bile that was threatening to gag him. "I must say, he looked better on their rap sheet…probably smelled better, too."

Tom made retching sounds, and backed away. "All we've got from finding Mike's car are just more unanswered questions. Who drove the car here after Mike was left dead in the ditch and, if it turns out that the man is indeed Harold, how did mother and son end up in its trunk?"

157

"It was an old picture of the two of them, but I'm quite sure that's Harold." Mitch's face, which had been chalk-white, suddenly filled with life. "Think! Mrs. Fuller remembered that Mike told her he was bringing Bernard with him to the book signing."

"Yes," Tom replied. "If I remember right, wasn't Mike wearing a tuxedo?"

"Yes, he was. It was a formal affair, kicking off Mrs. Fuller's first book in her new series."

"And wasn't there a piece of heavy material caught on a tree branch across the street where the killer stood?"

"Yes, and wouldn't that be someone in formal attire also?"

"That's what the evidence pointed to. So where does that leave us?"

"That leads us straight to Bernard!" Mitch reasoned. "Bernard killed Mike on the way to the book sighing!"

Cheers and high-fives filled the woods. Things quieted down when Tom asked, "Are you gonna tell us why he killed Mike? And why are mother and maybe her son sharing trunk space?"

Silence.

In the quiet, Tom's ringing cell phone sounded harsh.

"Hello? What did you say? What?"

Tom's face, when he turned around, was so white his freckles matched the red of his hair. "Marie's water broke!" he cried.

Marie, a nurse, had been in the room when Tom had awakened after being stabbed by Sammy the Grunt at a Sunday open house. Tom's first thought when he'd gazed into Marie's beautiful face was that she was an angel. In his muddled thinking, if he was seeing an angel, that meant he was dead.

Even though he'd been teased unmercifully about his mistake, he hadn't changed his mind about Marie. And now his angel was about to give birth to their child.

"What do I do? What do I do?" he yelled, his green eyes pleading for answers.

"Calm down," Mitch said quietly. "Take my car and go. I'll find a ride back with one of your men. Go!"

"B-b-but what about that?" Tom stammered as he pointed to the car's trunk that was stuffed with dead people.

"We'll take care of it. Marie needs you, so go!" Mitch handed Tom the keys to his car, then put his hands on Tom's shoulders and turned him towards the path that would take him to the car parked on the two-track. "Go!"

THE CAR SENT to pick up Bernard sat outside the house for ten minutes before the agent tried calling the house's phone number. When, after repeated attempts, no one picked up the phone, he dialed the agency.

"Bernard is a no-show," he reported.

"Damn. We should have expected this. Is there any activity in the house that you can see?"

"Nothing. What do I do now?"

"Try ringing the door bell. If no one answers, then see if the door is unlocked."

"You want me to go in?"

"Yes. Keep me on the line."

Nothing more was said until the agent spoke into his cell phone. "The door was unlocked and the house is empty. His packed bag is here, but no Bernard."

"Damn!"

"You think our boy met with foul play? What are the chances that George got suspicious? Bernard was acting pretty weird."

"We never should have given Bernard any time. He was at the cracking point yesterday."

"What does that mean for us? Do we have to speed things up in case George plans on skipping?"

"I say we just wait and watch. We should know soon enough if George is wise to us. Just leave."

CHAPTER 35

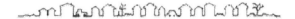

FIRE CHIEF JOE SKINNER had just returned to the station with his crew after answering an alarm from one of the local grade schools. The principal of the school had reported that, for a few seconds, an alarm had been set off somewhere in the building, but had then stopped. The fire department, which was just a few blocks from the school, arrived within minutes to see the orderly evacuation of the classrooms. The school was empty with the exception of the problem boy in Mrs. Bell's fourth grade class. He was standing in the hall with his hand on the fire alarm box.

Mrs. Bell, seeing that the kid's hand was still on the box yelled, "Get away from there! You've caused enough problems."

The kid was pretty sure that if he took his hand away and the lid flopped down, the alarm would ring again.

"Did you hear me!"

Shrugging, he dropped his hand. The lid flopped down, and the alarm rang again. Ignoring the din, the mischief-maker walked away with a satisfied smile on his face. He had always wondered what would happen if he pulled down on the fire alarm box; now he knew.

Joe, who hadn't forgotten some of his own youthful pranks, was still chuckling when his cell phone rang.

"Hello, my wife. And to what do I owe the pleasure of your call?"

"Our dog is out and headed in your direction. Call me when he gets there."

"I'll do better than that. I'll go outside and wait for him. Just stay on the line and talk to me. He should be here in a couple of minutes."

"Ha, it's nice that some people have jobs that give them time off to wait for a dog." Clara teased.

"Oh, have you checked on your sister, Marie, lately?"

"Why? Have you heard something?"

"Yeah. Her water broke."

"Marie's in labor?"

"Would seem so."

"Where did you hear it?"

"I talked to one of the policemen who was with Tom today when they found Mike's car."

"Mike's car? The Mike who was in the ditch with our Anita?"

"Yes, that Mike. Seems there were two dead people in the trunk."

"Come on now! Really? Are you making this up just so you won't be bored while waiting for Lucky to show up?"

"No, my love, I'm not making it up. I'm surprised Molly hasn't called you. One of the dead people is Mrs. Kingham, or whatever her name really is. The other one they think is her son, Harold. It's still a mystery who killed them or how they ended up in Mike's trunk."

"Oh, my goodness! This has to be a true story because I don't believe you have the imagination to make up something like this."

"Hey, wait a minute!"

"Let's get back to my sister. What have you heard that I don't know?"

"I'm going to ignore the fact that my wife just insulted me," Joe sniffed. "Anyhow, they had just found the bodies when Tom got a call on his cell phone. Marie's water had broken and Tom rushed off to the hospital."

"Oh, my little sister is having a baby and I'm going to be an aunt! I'd really like to close the office and head for the hospital, but I can't. I can call Tom on his cell phone, though. Hey, has Lucky shown up?"

"No, I haven't seen him and he should be here by now. That dog! What's he up to now?"

"I guess if we really want to know, we're going to have to follow him. As long as he comes back on schedule, I'm not going to worry about him. He's a big dog and he can take care of himself."

———————

REDHEADED, GREEN-EYED Tom Allen gazed down at the redheaded blue-eyed seven-pound baby in his arms. Love that he had never before known engulfed his body. The baby's waving hand made contact with one of Tom's fingers and latched on. Tom thought his heart was going to burst.

Marie stirred. "Are you supporting his head, Tom?" she mumbled. "Gotta support his head." Her eyes closed, and she fell back to sleep.

Tom backed into the rocking chair and sat down; they were still in the recovery room. He knew somewhere in the hospital both their mothers were waiting to see what their new grandson looked like. They could wait; this was his moment.

———————

GEORGE LOOKED PUZZLED. "I don't understand this. Where's Bernard?" He was standing inside his brother's bedroom going through a bag that contained Bernard's belongings.

"Looks like he was planning on going somewhere," Ted observed. "Any idea where that might be?"

"No, because he has nowhere to go. I'm the only family he has, plus he has no money of his own. Have you noticed that he's been acting a bit strange lately?"

Ted swallowed a snort. Noticed it? George must be blind not to have seen Bernard's reaction every time he winked at him. Harold, wherever he was, was threatening Bernard for some reason. Maybe if he found Bernard, he'd find Harold and his mother, too.

The meeting George had taken him to today finally revealed the family business. By pretending to be Harold, he had gotten himself mixed up in wide network of medical fraud. Doctors, clinics, nursing and assisted living homes, pharmacists, and dentists were included in the list of participating medical professionals. The raping of Medicare had to be in the billions.

A thought made Ted grin; maybe he was more like Anita than like the rest of his family. He'd played along with his mother and Harold, and look where it had gotten him. The promise he had made to himself while in prison was that once he got out, he was never going back. The business George was in was a sure ticket to prison; the network was too vast, there were too many people involved, and the reward for whistle blowing was too enticing. The last thing Ted wanted was to be mixed up in medical fraud. All he wanted to do was to get the ring and then disappear. He was deep in thought when the doorbell rang.

"I'll get it!" yelled George with a relieved voice. "Wanna bet it's Bernard? He's always forgetting his key."

Expecting to see Bernard when he threw open the door, the "Oh!" that he managed to utter sounded strangled.

The man standing in the open doorway holding a badge had the face of someone bearing serious news. George's heart skipped a beat. Had the officials stumbled onto his network? Had one of his recruits been a plant? Fear took away his power to speak.

"I'm Detective Hatch," said the man with the badge. " I'm looking for George Wing."

His dry mouth refused to form words. Was this the end? Who squealed? He grabbed the edge of the door to support his trembling legs. "I-I-I'm George Wing."

"Do you employ a Harold Foreman?"

"Yes," George managed to say. "Yes, I do have a man by that name working for me. What's this about?"

Mitch hated it when he had to relate bad news. He took a deep breath, and said, "I'm sorry to have to tell you this, but Harold Foreman is dead."

George's eyes were wild with relief. The detective wasn't here to arrest him. Letting out the breath he was holding, he could feel the release of tension as fear drained from his body.

"What did you just say?"

Mitch had watched the interesting display of emotions as they played over George's face. "I said Harold Foreman is dead."

What was the detective talking about? For heaven's sake, Harold had been with him all day and right now he was in the kitchen having a cup of coffee.

George shook his head and almost smiled. "That can't be! There's been a mistake."

"I'm sorry again, Mr. Wing, but we found Mike Fuller's car. He worked for you, too, didn't he?"

"Wait a minute! You found Mike's car?"

"Yes, we found Mike's car."

"That's great, but what does finding Mike's car have to do with Harold who you say is dead?"

"Harold and his mother were in the trunk."

"That can't be!" George again declared. He turned his back on the detective and yelled into the house. "Harold, will you come here a minute?"

"What's up?" Ted asked as he joined George at the door.

"Harold, this detective says you and your mother were found dead in the trunk of a car. Want to explain?"

Ted's face turned white.

Mitch's was still struggling with George Wing, who was intent on getting his hands around the throat of the man who had claimed to be Harold, but according to the man himself, was not Harold, when back-up arrived.

Ted Foreman looked none the worse for wear as he sat in Mitch's office. In fact, he looked relieved.

"Want to explain this mess?" Mitch asked.

"It just happened," shrugged Ted. "Harold, my brother, had written to me while I was still in prison. He was supposed to be waiting for me when I got off the prison bus. But Harold never showed up, and now I know why." Ted paused, to take a deep breath. "I was told that Mom was working as a live-in to a family named Hatch. Is that you?"

Mitch nodded. "That's my family. She took the identity of a woman who had died in George Wing's assisted living home. We hired her to help us with infant twins."

Ted snorted. "Mom hated babies! She didn't even like her own!"

"Unfortunately, we found that out," Mitch sighed. "Mr. Foreman, we think we know, but I'd like to hear your version of what your mother thought she was doing."

"She was looking for a ring. Before Aunt Jennie died, she had given Anita a very valuable ring. Since it was worth a lot of money, Harold probably talked Mom into doing the live-in thing, thinking she'd be able to find the ring if she stayed in the room where Anita had lived."

Mitch just shook his head. "Why didn't she just tell us she was Anita's mother and ask for the ring? The girls were using it as a toy."

"It was probably Harold's idea. He got his jollies just thinking he was outsmarting someone."

"How did you become Harold?"

"George did that. He thought I was Harold, and since Harold hadn't shown up, I just went along with it. But his brother, Bernard, didn't. He was terrified of me. I could make him vomit just by looking at him and nodding my head in a knowing way. What was that all about?"

"We think Bernard killed Harold and then stuffed him into the trunk of Mike's car. Seeing you was probably making him doubt his sanity."

"W-w-why did he kill my brother?"

"That we don't know."

"And Mom? Do you know how she ended up in the same trunk?"

Mitch shook his head. "No idea."

"Anita, Mom, Harold…my entire family gone," Ted groaned, his head bowed.

Not knowing how to respond, Mitch didn't say anything.

Raising his head, Ted asked, "Where is Bernard?"

"There's an all-points bulletin out on him. Someone's going to find him."

The two sat in silence.

Ted cleared his throat. "About the ring."

Mitch didn't hesitate. "It was quite by accident that we found out it wasn't a play ring, but a valuable real one. Since then, it's been in a safety-deposit box at the bank. Mr. Foreman, the ring is yours."

Ted was uncertain as to the next move. George Wing was running a very successful run on Medicare. Should he become an informant and spend the rest of his life trying to stay one step ahead of George's contract goons, or should he take the ring and run? When he thought of it that way, was there even a choice?

Mitch looked at the man who was Anita's brother. At one point in their conversation, Mitch had gotten the feeling that Ted was about to tell him something. He had an eagerness about him that Mitch had seen before in witnesses when they were about to reveal a secret. The moment passed and the feeling fled; Ted knew something, but he wasn't going to talk.

With a sad expression on his face, Ted asked, "I'd like to talk about the two dead people, my mother, and my brother, Harold. What's going to happen to their bodies? Do I have to identify them?"

"I identified your mother, and George has identified Harold, so you are spared that job. I don't think you'd want to remember your family the way they looked after weeks in the trunk. They're in the morgue right now waiting autopsies. You were in prison when Anita was murdered. Were you told?"

"Harold wrote to me, but it was weeks after the funeral." Ted cleared his throat to hide a sob. "Anita, well, what can I say about a sister who was born knowing right from wrong? Harold and I went along with Mom because we thought that's what families did. But Anita knew better, right from the start."

"Mr. Foreman, we loved your sister. Losing her created a hole in our lives and in our family. Molly rushed home when we found out who our Mrs. Kingham really was, not just to confront her about her deceitful identity, but to ask questions about Anita. By the time we got home, your mother was gone."

Ted laughed softly. "Anita stuck out like a bandaged thumb in our family. Mom never could figure out where she came from. Would your wife like to ask me the questions she never got to ask Mom?"

Mitch nodded. "Molly has her own business, Allen Real Estate. She had to take the twins to work with her today because we haven't found anyone to replace your mother. Would you mind going with me to her office?"

Ted grinned. "I'd love to be able to talk about Anita. She tried her best to make me see her view of life, but Mom was stronger."

Mitch picked up the phone and called Molly.

CHAPTER 36

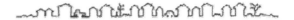

JOE CLEARED HIS desk, put on his coat, and was about to walk out the door when he remembered the dog. It had been a busy day and after Clara had dismissed the idea that they should worry about Lucky because 'he was a big dog and could take care of himself', he hadn't given the dog a thought. But now that he had, he picked up the phone and called Clara at her office. She had the car with the fire truck trailer attached that would be needed to transport Lucky home.

"Hello, Allen Real Est..."

"It's me, Clara. Did Lucky show up?"

"You mean at my office? No, he left to go to your office hours ago. Remember?"

"Well, he never got here."

Silence.

"Joe, what do we do now?"

"He has to be within walking distance. How hard will it be to find a dog that big?"

"He's always back here in time to ride home on the trailer. I'll stay here in case he's just late. Why don't you drive around and look for him? Call me when you find him and I'll come with the trailer."

"I'm leaving right now."

The digital clock showed 3:15 A.M. Joe had moved to the couch to get away from Clara's sobs. Nothing he had done had quieted her. If he himself hadn't loved Lucky so much, he might be feeling jealous of the

170

big dog. His secret hope was that Clara loved him as much as she loved the mutt.

Morning found him still on the couch. Grabbing his pillow, he joined Clara in bed; she groaned when he crawled in beside her. Dawn's ugly light revealed dark circles of exhaustion around Clara's red-rimmed eyes.

The ringing phone awakened feelings of hope; maybe someone had seen their famous dog and was calling to tell them where he was. Clara won the race to the phone. "Hello?" she said in an expectant voice.

"Good morning, Aunt Clara!" Tom yelled. "I'm a dad!"

Her shoulders sagged; she looked at Joe and shook her head. However, it was good family news that Marie had delivered, so she took a deep breath, plastered a fake smile on her face, and exclaimed, "Well, how about that! What did you get and how is my sister?"

"We got a seven-pound redheaded boy! Oh, and Marie is still sleeping, but the doctor said she's fine. Just tired."

"Have a name for your boy?"

"Not yet. Marie said if we live with him awhile, he'll tell us what he wants to be called."

"I really don't think you can wait that long," Clara chuckled. "Maybe, in a few days when you get to know him, the right name will come."

"Clara, is everything all right? You sound different."

"Tom, everything's not all right. Lucky's missing. Yesterday he left my office to go to the fire station, but he never showed up."

"That's not like Lucky at all! Think someone poisoned him again?"

"Oh, my! I never thought of that! Joe," she called. "Tom's a dad!"

"Congratulations!" Joe yelled back.

"Tom just asked if we thought someone might have poisoned Lucky again. Had you thought of that?"

"No, that never entered my mind. I just figured when he hadn't been showing up at my office in the afternoons that maybe he had found another home. I never mentioned it to you because I knew how upset you would be. But he was going somewhere. We just have to find where."

Clara wailed. "My dog found another home? How can he do this to me?" Dropping the phone, she ran into the bathroom."

"Hello? Hello? Anybody there?"

Joe climbed out of bed and picked up the phone. "You still there, Tom?"

"Yes, I'm still here. What happened to Clara?"

"She's in the bathroom bawling. All I can say is, Lucky had better have a pretty good story when he does show up!"

"But what if he doesn't?" asked Tom.

"Don't even think about it! He's got to be within walking distance. Gotta go, Tom. But, again, congratulations!"

MITCH STUDIED THE young man who had just placed a bag on top of his desk. The name sewed on the pocket of his shirt identified him.

"Bob, tell me again where you found this."

"It was stuck on the branch of a tree that I was trimming. You know, the big intersection going out of town?"

Mitch knew what intersection he was talking about. The city had routinely kept the trees trimmed ever since the fatal accident that had been caused by a motorist's inability to see through low branches.

The last time he had seen this bag was the day he and Molly had watched the woman they had hired climb out of a taxi and walk up their driveway. He was looking at Agnes Foreman's bag.

CHAPTER 37

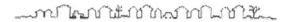

EMILY FULLER'S FINGERS were flying over the computer's keys finishing a chapter in the second book of her series, when her fingers stopped mid-sentence. Mike's last statement had just popped unbidden into her brain. She had laughed when he had said it because it was an unusual thing for Mike to say. Had she remembered something important? Should she even bother Detective Hatch with such a silly statement?

Emily reached for the phone, and then changed her mind; Mitch Hatch had more important things to worry about.

Why weren't her fingers moving? What had happened to the story line? Emily gave up. Her stories were character driven, and for some reason, the characters weren't cooperating. She reached for the phone.

Mitch sat with the phone still in his hand and wondered if Emily Fuller had supplied a piece to the puzzle he was trying to solve. All fingers pointed to Bernard as Mike's killer, but there had never been a clue as to what would cause Bernard, who had liked Mike, to kill him.

According to Emily, Mike had told her that he was bringing Bernard to her book signing because he wanted time alone with Bernard. His actual words were, "I need to have a 'come to Jesus' meeting with Bernard."

What did Mike know about Bernard that fueled a situation that ended with Mike dead in a ditch? Mitch remembered that Bernard had tried to lure Billy to his car. Had Bernard been successful in enticing other young boys and Mike knew about it? He had been told that because of Bernard's perversions, George Wing hadn't allowed his brother to be a part of the family business. Had Mike threatened to tell George what he had discovered?

Presuming he had figured out Mike's murder, that still left the Harold and Agnes puzzle. The autopsy revealed that Harold had been shot with the same gun that had killed Mike. If Bernard was Mike's killer, that would place Harold's death on him, too. There was no motive for that one because Bernard and Harold hadn't known each other.

The autopsy on Agnes revealed that she had been struck by something heavy, probably a car. That much was known even before her bag was found atop a tree at the busy intersection. How she got from there to the trunk of Mike's car was still a mystery.

Bernard again? Had Bernard been a one-man exterminating machine? Mitch took all his facts to a judge and obtained a warrant to search George Wing's car.

George was feeling guilty. He had promised their mother on her deathbed that he would take care of his younger brother. Bernard had been missing for days now, and the feeling George had was one of relief. That's why he was feeling guilty.

Bernard had always been more of a thorny pain in the ass rather than a brother to love. George felt liberated. No longer did he have to keep an eye on Bernard's activities. He cringed at the knowledge that even after he had threatened Bernard,, he had still found child porn hidden in Bernard's room. George hated uncomfortable situation; he hadn't confronted Bernard with his find.

Everything was running smoothly; his network was expanding. Except for a few brief instances when either Medicare or the FBI Fraud investigators had him in their crosshairs, no one was giving his activities a second look. Life was good.

When the doorbell rang, he answered it with a smile on his face. One look at the police officer wiped away the smile.

"Mr. Wing?" asked the officer.

George paused for a second, wondering what would happen if he claimed to be someone else.

"That's me. What's this about?"

"We have a warrant to search your car, Mr. Wing."

"My car? What about my car?"

"This is a warrant that gives us the right to search your car."

"I heard you the first time. Does this have anything to do with me?"

"Where is the car, Mr. Wing? I need the keys."

George was so relieved that the warrant was for his car and not his house, he handed the officer the keys without another word. In his thinking, he had done nothing wrong that involved his car. Did this have something to do with Bernard?

Back when Bernard had cleaned the car after he'd hit and killed Agnes Foreman, he thought he'd done away with all the evidence. However, the crime lab found traces of blood on the back seat that matched Agnes' blood type. An almost undetectable dent in the roof of the car spoke volumes.

Barnard had been a one-man killing machine.

CHAPTER 38

CLARA GAVE THE woman with uncombed hair, mismatched clothes, and hunched shoulders a critical stare until she realized it was her own reflection in the store's window. Straightening her shoulders, she pushed hair out of red-rimmed eyes and looked around for the next spot to attach a lost-dog poster. Every evening for the past week she'd plastered the poster in areas within walking distance of her office. Lucky had ridden on his trailer to her office that last morning. He had slept the morning away on his bed in the office and, after a noon snack, she had sent him on his way to visit Joe at the fire station. But he had never arrived, and he hadn't been seen since; she was offering a reward.

The atmosphere in the office of Allen Real Estate was tense. Molly was bringing both teething babies to work with her; some days all that Clara and Molly did during the working hours was tend to the babies. When one baby slept, the other one howled. Guilty feelings didn't stop Clara from leaving Molly alone with the twins while she disappeared for hours, walking the streets, calling Lucky, and tacking up posters. Thinking that maybe Lucky would pick tonight to show up and need a ride home, she hung around the office long after closing hours. Joe and the boys hadn't had a cooked meal in days.

Streetlights were coming on by the time Clara rounded the corner on the way back to her office. She had used all the posters and, before tomorrow, she would have to make more. Deep in thought, she almost ran into a woman who was in the process of attaching a picture of a small white dog over one of Lucky's posters.

"Hey, lady, watch what you're doing!" she called as she hurried her steps. "That's my dog you're covering up!"

The woman gave Clara a guilty glance. "Sorry about that," she muttered.

"Lose your dog, too?" asked Clara.

"Yes," the woman nodded as she wiped her nose with a tissue, "and I'm just sick about it. Syndee is my baby, and she needs me!"

Clara looked at the poster that proclaimed Syndee, a professionally groomed little dog with painted nails and a bow in her hair, was lost. S-y-n-d-e-e was Cindy? The dog was one pampered pooch; no, you'd better make that one registered-pedigreed-pampered-pooch.

"That's a…ah,…that's a good looking dog," Clara lied.

"Too bad I can't say that about yours," sneered the woman. "That's one of the ugliest mutts I've ever seen."

Clara whirled on the lady. "Watch your mouth! Lucky is special!"

"Not special enough to be around my little darling!" the woman huffed as she tore down her poster and walked away.

"My dog is better than your dog!" Clara was yelling as Joe came up behind her.

"What in the world is going on?" he chuckled. "You two women fighting over your dogs?"

"What she has isn't even a dog," Clara muttered. "It's a plaything. A useless plaything! Lucky is worth a hundred times more than her pampered little yip-yap!"

"Are you out of posters, too?" Joe asked, trying to change the subject.

"Yes. I'll make more tomorrow. Where are the boys?"

"At home. I ran into old friends today who had their daughter with them. She's in college and needs money to buy books for next semester, so I invited her home to sit with the boys. They were all watching television when I left."

"You left our boys with a stranger?"

"I wouldn't call her a stranger, exactly. Anyway, I knew I was going to be gone just for a bit. I think it's time for us both to go home. Lucky doesn't want to be found."

———————

THE PET STORE manager yawned. It was closing time and he'd had a busy day. Was it time for him to eat crow and apologize to his new salesperson? Contrary to what he had predicted was going to happen, the dog food hadn't been stolen, the neighboring stores hadn't complained about the barking dogs, and the dogs hadn't killed each other. Ed's idea of an outdoor display had been a howling success. Bags of dog food, one of them split-open, placed high out of reach of several employee's fenced-in dogs had brought laughing customers into his store all day.

He watched as Ed dismantled the display after the howling dogs had gone home with their owners at closing time. Ed had removed the three full bags from the display and placed them by the door while he worked at cleaning up the spilled food from the split bag.

When the manager looked out again, he saw Ed standing by the door, scratching his head. "Something wrong?" he called to Ed.

"I swear I had three full bags."

"You did," assured the manager. "I saw them."

"So why are there only two now?"

"One is missing? I haven't seen any activity around the door."

"The small ten pound bag is gone."

"How about that? Maybe a kid stole it to feed his dog."

Ed looked contrite. "I'm sorry I wasn't paying attention. I'll pay for…"

The manager laughed. "You're not paying for anything, Ed. Your idea paid for that bag many times over. I just hope the kid who snitched it has a guilty conscience for the rest of his life!"

––––––––––

THE SUNDAY'S EDITION of the town's only paper had a big article about Lucky, the celebrity dog that had gone missing.

Clara had been interviewed and quoted extensively, but the pictures were all from the newspaper's archives. One of the first pictures was of Lucky sitting on top of the evil Santa he had brought to justice. The next one showed him sitting on top of the wicked Sammy the Grunt who he had run down in a vineyard. He was a sad-looking mangy dog in the next picture. Sitting beside the grave of a murder victim, his missing fur and bare patches of skin were, according to the paper, related to yet another story. Lucky had thrown his body over Joe, one of his owners, protecting him from an exploding bomb. There was a funny one taken at Joe and Clara's wedding. Joe cringed when he opened the paper at the breakfast table and saw it.

"You're never going to live that down!" Clara said from behind him.

Joe jumped. "Didn't hear you sneak up on me."

"Did they quote me correctly?" she asked, trying to read over Joe's shoulder.

"Here, you take it. I have an early meeting at work."

He left Clara sitting alone at the table, crying over the article. Each picture she looked at brought a fresh load of tears. Where was her dog?

Lucky had to be within walking distance. Why didn't he just come home? The thought that he had found a home he liked better than with her, the boys and Joe was devastating. Clara put her head down on the table and sobbed.

CHAPTER 39

WHERE WAS BERNARD?

George Wing was past being relieved that Bernard wasn't around to cause him headaches. The man had just vanished, leaving behind a fully packed bag. Whatever the kid had in mind, he was planning on being away from home a long time. Since he had no car and no money, there had to be other people involved in Bernard's disappearance.

The two-Harold incident still had him shaking his head. His first reaction to Ted, who was pretending to be Harold, was a violent one. In his mind, Ted was posing as Harold for some nefarious reason. Maybe a plant? The police had roughed him up a bit when they pried his fingers from around Ted's neck. That was the last he had seen of the man. Rumors were that Ted was seen coming out of the bank right before he boarded a bus headed out of town.

Another puzzling thing was the interest the police had in finding Bernard. He'd like to find him, too, but the police wanted him in connection with Mike's murder. What would make them think he would have anything to do with Mike's killing? Bernard had really liked Mike.

Removing articles one by one from the bag, George uncovered Bernard's laptop computer. It had been carefully nestled among the clothes, its power cord still attached. His computer was no stranger to George. A very young Bernard's visits to objectionable sites on the Internet had resulted in George placing restrictive blocks on those sites. Since Bernard had constantly found ways around those blocks, George had made periodical inspections. Hoping that Bernard had been too lazy to change the password, he plugged in the dangling cord and turned on the computer.

As he sat at his desk watching Bernard's computer come to life, he had mixed feelings. Was he going to find out something about his brother that he'd rather not know? Since early childhood, Bernard had been different. The family chose to ignore the signs, pretending that if no one acknowledged the problem, then there wasn't one. George knew better. Had Bernard met someone on the Internet who shared his perversion? Had that someone done something terrible to Bernard?

George's first stop was the Internet where he found the sites that Bernard had visited prior to his vanishing.

Medical and Medicare fraud sites popped up. George smiled. Bernard was finally getting interested in the family business. Maybe there was hope for the kid, after all.

His smile vanished when he visited the next two sites, Witness Protection Agency and Reward for Whistle Blowing. Another site struck fear into his heart. Step by step, the article outlined what had to be done to get accepted into the Witness Protection Program.

From the Internet, George went to Bernard's e-mail. Since he had no friends, Bernard hadn't sent too many e-mails. None of the few that he had sent or received contained anything that interested him.

From e-mail, George went to Bernard's documents and clicked to open the last saved one. George stared at the screen.

With whom had Bernard shared this list? Paralyzing fear filled his body. He was dead. Everyone on this list was dead. How could Bernard do this to him? He prayed that the perverted friend from the Internet wouldn't kill Bernard; George wanted to. His fingers itched to squeeze Bernard's fleshy neck. Then it hit him. Bernard wasn't off with someone he had met on the Internet; he'd been picked up by the Feds. His brother was now in protective services!

The little pervert was a whistleblower!

George's mind ran in crazed circles. What should he do? Alert everyone on the list that the game was over? He thought of all the professionals he had talked into the scheme. Just by reporting a procedure as minor as treating an ingrown toenail as an operation that completely removed the nail was so easy to do. When people got their Medicare information, the chance that an older person would even read the report let alone find something wrong with it was a chance they were willing to take. It was a chance that paid off in billions.

Was there a way for him to get out of this? Remembering the site with information on how to become a whistleblower, his fingers flew over the computer keys. He knew more about his network than Bernard had put on his list. What if he became a whistleblower?

His eye caught the same statement that had sent Bernard down the path to become an informer. In Bernard's case, he needed the money. In George's case, he needed to save his life.

If the Justice Department wins the case with information given to them by the whistleblower, the whistleblower is entitled to a maximum of 25% of any recovered money.

The information he had on his network would be worth millions! Maybe he and Bernard could live together after all. With new names, a new location, and all that money, life would be good!

That was, of course, after he'd had the pleasure of feeling his fingers squeezing Bernard's soft fleshy neck.

CHAPTER 40

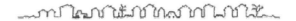

"BUT I DON'T want to go!" sobbed Clara.

Joe pulled Clara to him and hugged her hard. "We've got to keep on living, hon. I'm heartbroken, too, but life goes on, no matter how it hurts!"

"Please! I want to put up more posters tonight. That crazy lady is taking mine down and putting up pictures of her ugly pretend-dog."

"I'll do it for you...I promise. Now go get ready."

"I shouldn't have let you talk me into this, Joe. I didn't like those kids when I was in high school, so what makes you think I'll like them any better as adults? I don't want to go to this damn reunion."

Joe sighed. "I'm sorry, but I thought it was important. Every time we talk about our high school experiences, you cringe. It's as if it's a period in your life you don't even want to think about."

"You've got that right! I spent those four years hiding. I didn't join anything so who's even going to remember me?"

"Just go back, for me. I want you to be able to erase all those negative memories and replace them with good ones. You're going to outshine everyone there! Now, go put on your new dress; I want to be the first one to see you in it."

"Too late for that! I've already modeled it for Molly."

Joe laughed. "So, I'm happy to be the second one to see you in it!"

Clara sat alone at a long table. A tag plastered onto her new dress shouted her name. People she could swear she had never seen before paraded past her. Men with bald heads and expanded waists looked her over with glad eyes. Well, now, that was different. No male in her entire four years of high school had ever looked at her that way. She was amused to see that girls who had caught the boys' eyes with their early maturing now looked matronly. Clara grinned. Maybe Joe knew what he was talking about.

"Something funny?" asked a male voice. While she had been checking her classmates, a man had taken the seat beside her at the table.

Clara turned to look at him. The man, whose one-time muscled body was turning to flab, looked familiar. He did remind her of someone, but she had to look at his nametag to see that he was...Bill. Her eyes widened. Bill, the most popular guy for the entire four years and the football captain to boot was talking to her.

Flustered, she put herself back onto the bottom rung of the old high school pecking order. Why was the most popular kid in school talking to her? She couldn't come up with words.

Looking at her nametag, Bill squinted. "I don't seem to remember you. Were you in any of my classes?"

Clara nodded.

"Are you sure? How could I have missed someone as beautiful as you?"

How indeed?

"I-I remember you, though," Clara stammered, her heart pounding. "You were pretty hard to miss those four years."

"Those were the best years of my life," Bill replied softly.

The best years of his life? Clara winced just thinking about those years.

"What have you done since graduation?" she asked, thinking his answer was going to be something great. Bill had been at the top of everything. From being the homecoming king to the president of all his classes, she was sure that today he was probably a brain surgeon or a rocket scientist, or the CEO of a big company…better yet, the owner of a big comp….

"I sell vacuum cleaners" he replied. "I'm a door-to-door salesman."

Clara stammered. "R-r-really?" Even though he hadn't measured up to her expectations, she was still having problems talking to the boy she had so admired for those four years. What to say now?

"Ah, do you ever sell in the area of Allen Real Estate? That's where I work."

"So," he said as his eyes returned to her face, "if you work in a real estate office, does that mean you sell houses?"

Clara nodded.

Bill slid across the bench and whispered into her ear, "Honey, someone as pretty as you could talk me into buying anything!"

Clara cringed. Is this what she had missed in high school?

"Darlin'," Bill sighed as he gazed into her eyes. "I wish my territory covered your area. I'd love to stop by Allen Real Estate and have a cup of coffee with you. We could talk about the good old days!"

Every good salesperson quickly learns the facial grimaces of rejection, and since Bill was a good salesperson, Clara's face was speaking to him loud and clear. He swallowed hard and changed the subject. "My buddy Mike has that part of town. My route is the west side."

Suddenly, he tilted his head to look at her more closely. "Haven't I seen your picture in the paper along with a really big dog?"

"Yeah, you have," Clara felt relief that the sticky part of their conversation was over. "My dog Lucky has made the front page of the paper several times. In fact, did you see today's paper?"

"No, I didn't have time to read the paper this morning. But do you still have that dog?"

"What makes you ask?"

"Because I saw him the other day."

Clara jumped up from the table. "You saw Lucky? He's been gone for days! Where did you see him?"

"He was on one of the side streets in my area. He wasn't looking too good, now that I think about it."

"Not looking good? Oh, my God! What was wrong with him?"

"Well, for one thing, he was limping."

"Limping? My dog's limping? He needs me! I need to go find him. Please! Can you remember what side street? He won't get into a car, so wherever you saw him, he walked there."

Bill fumbled in his pocket, looking for a piece of paper. "I'd draw you a map if we can come up with paper...and a pen. Do you have either?"

Clara looked at her small bag she had brought to the reunion. The fact that it matched her dress wasn't making her like it any better right now; there was nothing in it but lipstick and the keys to her car.

Pulling a pen out of an inner pocket, Bill exclaimed, "Here we go! We're half-way there!"

Clara rolled up her sleeve and held out her arm. "Here. Draw a map."

Bill hesitated. "I have the feeling that as soon as I draw the map, you're out of here?"

"You've got that right!"

Bill shrugged in resignation and went to work.

Not wanting to smear his map, Clara waited for a few seconds before she pulled down her sleeve. Rushing back to her room, she packed, checked out of the hotel, and with never a backward glance, ran for her car.

CHAPTER 41

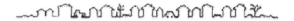

THE SMALL OFFICE of Allen Real Estate was packed. Molly had brought the twins into work with her, and since the school teachers were having a planning day, Laurie and Kim tagged along.

Sitting at the front desk answering the phone was Peggy Allen, mother of Molly and Tom. Peggy had stepped in to help many times in the past. Today she was here to fill in for Clara who was out looking for Lucky in a different part of town. Another reason was that Tom had said he was bringing the new baby, her grandson, into the office to be admired.

The volume of noise lowered as the office door swung open. All eyes turned to the door, expecting to see Tom and the new baby. The noise rose to a new level when Marilyn Hatch, Molly's mother-in-law, stepped into the office..

"A party, and I wasn't invited?" she laughed. "Someone's birthday?"

Molly greeted her with a struggling baby in each arm. "Have one," she said to Marilyn. "Please."

Marilyn looked at the squirming pair who appeared so innocent. She had heard from her son, Mitch, that the teething duo had kept the entire Hatch household awake last night with their demands.

"So," Marilyn asked them, "which one of you is the leader? Is it you, Thomas? Are you the one who decides when to let the family sleep? Or is it you, Jill?"

The twins squirmed, kicked their feet, and struggled to get down. "Oh, for heaven's sake, Marilyn, just take one of them! My arms are numb! Their teeth can't come in fast enough to suit me."

"Looks like they'd rather be on the floor than in your arms," observed Marilyn as she reached for Tom.

"The floor is filthy! There's dog hair everywhere." Molly warned.

"A little dirt never hurt anyone," Marilyn replied as she sat Tom down. "Oh, I see what you mean. Thomas, quit chewing on that bone! That's Lucky's bone!"

Molly laughed loud and long. "Point made?"

Marilyn removed the bone from Tom's mouth and picked him up. "Any news about the owner of that bone? How long has he been gone?"

"Too long! Clara is devastated thinking that Lucky has chosen to live with someone else. She isn't working, and I can't work, either. Allen Real Estate is suffering."

"Where's Clara now?"

"She ran into a salesman at her high school reunion who told her he had seen her dog. His territory is past the city limits, miles from here. That's where she is today, walking those streets and putting up posters."

"That dog. Wonder what he's up to this time."

"Whatever it is, I hope it brings in business. We're dying on the vine right now."

This time, when the door opened, it was Tom that walked in. The baby was nestled inside a sling hanging around Tom's neck.

Grinning from ear-to-ear, he announced, "I present to you Logan Earl Allen!"

"My grandson!" yelled Peggy from the front desk.

The din that followed woke up Logan Earl Allen. His protesting cry filled the office. One by one, voices went silent, as it dawned on the loving viewers that the loud raucous noise that was piercing their eardrums was coming from the small bundle in the sling.

"Unbelievable!" Marilyn finally murmured.

"Wow!" exclaimed Molly.

"That hurts my ears!" cried Kim.

Tom proudly yelled over the noise. "Isn't it wonderful? My son has a big voice!"

"Do something!" yelled Laurie. "Please make him stop!"

Tom looked puzzled. "H-h-he's just crying. Haven't you ever heard a baby cry before?"

Peggy yelled, "Have you?"

Tom scratched his red head. "Come to think of it, this is the first baby I've ever been around."

Big Sister Molly laughed. "I'm just glad that kid is yours and not mine. Tell me Tom, have the neighbors complained?"

"Now that you mention it, the people in the apartment below us have been banging on the ceiling with something; probably a broom handle. You think they can hear Logan crying way down there?"

Marilyn snorted. "They're probably hearing that kid in the next county!"

The baby gave one last blast, burped, and went back to sleep.

"Thank God!" muttered Molly.

"Hey, wait a minute! That's my kid you're putting down. Are you telling me that he's louder than other babies?"

All heads in the room nodded.

"How about that!" chuckled the proud dad.

Trying to change the subject, Molly asked, "I see you finally picked a name. I kinda like it."

"Thanks. Marie came up with Logan. It was a character's name in the book she was reading when she went into labor."

"I know where the middle name came from," Molly offered. "It's a family name. Our dad had that middle name, and so did his dad. Good choice, Brother Tom!"

The office door swung open and Clara appeared in the doorway. She paused to look at the faces staring back at her, then threw up her hands.

"Nothing."

With that, she burst into tears and headed for the bathroom.

Laurie and Kim, who had grown to love the big dog, ran to Molly for comfort.

"She didn't find him," sobbed Kim.

"No, she didn't. But we know he's out there somewhere."

"Do you think he doesn't like us anymore?"

"Knowing that dog, he's up to something. We just have to wait to find out what it is."

"Aunt Molly?"

"What, Laurie?"

"If Lucky doesn't come back, can we get a dog of our own?"

Molly sighed. "Laurie, how could we add a dog to our family right now? Mitch and I are having trouble taking care of what we already have!"

"But you did say that if we could find a dog like Lucky, we could keep it?"

"Yes, I said that, and I meant it. If you can find another dog like Lucky, you can have it."

Molly grinned to herself. What was the chance of that ever happening?

CHAPTER 42

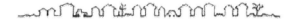

MITCH STOOD IN the doorway of the Omelet Shop, his eyes scanning the room looking for Tom. When he called him at home this morning, Marie had answered. Over earsplitting cries in the background, she had sarcastically snipped that "Some people get to go out for breakfast!"

On a table in the back of the room, Mitch saw a plate of sunny-side-up eggs, three strips of bacon, and a red head. As he got closer, he could hear a soft snore coming out of Tom's open mouth.

"I can see it all," Mitch announced in a loud voice. "The headline in the paper will read: A fully armed city policeman slept through a daring day-time robbery at the Omelet Shop."

"What? What? A robbery? Where?" yelled Tom. He jumped to his feet and knocked over his coffee.

When a frantic look around the room produced nothing out of the ordinary, Tom's eyes rested on Mitch's grinning face. "You bastard!" he muttered as he wiped the drool off his chin.

"Sorry about that." Mitch grabbed napkins and mopped up the spilled coffee. "I'll bet that was the most sleep you've gotten since Logan Earl's been born."

"You've got that right. I think we have to move."

"What? One seven-pound baby has crowded you out of your apartment?"

"It's the seven-pound baby's vocal cords that are getting us kicked out. When the landlord came calling this morning, we didn't even hear him pounding on the door because Logan was crying. Mitch, this kid has a great set of lungs on him."

"Whoa!" Mitch laughed. "I've heard new fathers boast about their new offspring for many reasons, but I've never heard one brag about vocal cords. Are you serious?"

"Afraid so. I had never been around a baby before, so I didn't know that Logan's cry was louder than other babies. But the neighbors have complained, and unless we can keep him quiet, we have to move."

"Well, you can't keep a baby quiet. Believe me, I've tried." Mitch was thinking about the nights he and Molly had walked the twins.

Tom managed a grin. "Wanna hear something funny?" Without waiting for Mitch to answer, he plowed on. "Joe's three boys were all excited when they heard Logan's middle name. Seems a dog by the name of Earl had lived at Jerry's foster home, and the boys thought we named our baby after the dog. I can't tell you how their faces fell when I explained that we had named our baby after a person and not a dog."

"Cute," Mitch nodded. "Eat."

"Now that I'm awake," Tom said between bites, "fill me in on what's going on. What have I missed?"

"Let's see. When you got the call about Marie, we had just gotten to the open trunk where we found Agnes Foreman and a man that I was pretty sure was Harold, her son."

"We had just figured out that Bernard had killed Mike when my phone rang. With all that evidence, did Bernard confess?"

"Bernard's gone. According to his brother, Bernard left a packed bag behind when he disappeared." Mitch paused to pull a crumpled piece of paper out of his pocket. Smoothing it out, he pointed to the face on it. "That's Bernard. There is an all-points bulletin on him."

Tom studied the picture. "He has to be around."

"What makes you say that?"

With a sheepish look on his face, Tom glanced around at the nearby tables before he admitted, "I got lost. You remember when you pointed me in the direction of the two-track road where your car was parked?"

Mitch nodded.

"I got mixed up in the middle of all those trees; I think I walked in circles. Marie needed me, and here I was, lost. I got so upset I didn't even see the bicycle until I stumbled over it and fell."

"So you found a bicycle. What does that have to do with Bernard?"

"It's Bernard's bike. There was an identification tag on it."

Mitch was getting excited. "We never did figure out why the trunk lid was up. Wanna bet Bernard was there already, and when he heard us coming, he ran into the woods?"

"Wanna hear about another bike?" Tom grinned.

"Another one?"

"Yes, another one. I picked myself up after falling over Bernard's bike, staggered a few feet into the trees, and tripped over another one. This one was in a bed of poison ivy. I got out of that patch real fast, so I don't know whose bike it was."

Mitch pulled out his cell phone.

"Who're you calling?"

"Detective Miller. He was assigned to the case at the beginning because I was too close to one of the victims; I didn't let that stop me. Detective Miller complained that I had taken over his case, which I had. When Emily Fuller gave me information and I didn't turn it over to him, he filed a complaint. I need to throw him a bone to shut him up."

Tom listened to Mitch explaining to Detective Miller why he should go to the clearing and look for the two bicycles.

When he closed his phone, Tom had a puzzled look on his face.

"Something the matter?" asked Mitch.

"Why didn't you tell him that while he was there he should look for Bernard?"

"That's because we're going to do it. Pay for your breakfast then let's get out of here."

"Aren't you doing it again?"

"What?"

"Stepping all over Miller's case?"

"I'm not going to worry about Miller unless we find something."

"Tom, you haven't told me about Agnes Foreman. Do you have any idea how she ended up in Mike's trunk?"

"Let's talk in the car. I'll tell you all about the tree-trimmer who found her bag in the branches of a tree."

"What?"

"Oh, and then there's the matter of two Harolds. That's quite a story!"

"What? What?"

"Patience, Tom. Let's get out of here."

CHAPTER 43

BROKENHEARTED CLARA slowly walked the route between her office and the fire station. Although she knew that Lucky was last seen miles from here, she still felt close to her dog in the familiar setting. Her solitary walk paused briefly when she saw the picture of pampered, pedigreed Syndee tacked over her Lucky poster. Tearing it down and crumbling it gave her a brief moment of emotional release.

What side street had he taken on all those afternoons when she thought he was with Joe at the station? At the next side street, she turned right and followed it until it met up with a busy highway. Lucky had never left her side when their walks encountered heavy traffic; he was smart enough to know danger when he saw it. Clara turned around and retraced her steps back to the familiar street.

She was a block from the station when she noticed a path that veered off the sidewalk and ran into a wooded area; she was sure that her dog's curiosity would lure him down that trail.

The treed area was not large; it was just a boundary between houses. Clara inspected the section, hoping the residences of the adjoining houses weren't watching. She was about to leave when her eye caught a flash of red. Turning around, she found herself in front of a hole dug out of a small rise in the ground. Around the hole were the remains of what was once a red bag of dog food. It had rained several times since Lucky had disappeared. Prints of his huge feet were embedded in the mud, along with much smaller prints.

Had Lucky found a friend?

WITH POSTERS OF her lost dog clutched in her hand, Eileen Weber retraced her steps. Her mission, to remove the lost dog notice about the ugly beast and replace it with pictures of her beautiful Syndee, was accomplished. The thought of that ugly mutt's picture being close to her darling gave her the shivers. She was sure it had been bred into Syndee never to associate with such trash.

Syndee had been gone for so long! Where was her angel?

MITCH PARKED HIS car by the path off the two-track road.

"What if Detective Miller comes while we're here? Think we should hide your car?" asked Tom.

"He didn't sound too enthusiastic about the lead I gave him. I'd be surprised if he even follows up on it."

"He's that kind of detective?"

"Yeah, a lazy one. We can check out the other bicycle while we're here in case he doesn't."

"Ah, Mitch," Tom muttered, "are you real sure of how to get back to the clearing? Remember, I got lost in there, really lost! Man, I hate that feeling."

"I have it all figured out; stick with me. Remember those bear tracks and the piles of scat? One thing we don't want to do is get between a mother and her cub. In Michigan, we don't have man-eating grizzlies, but our black bears will attack if they're worried about their young."

The clearing was empty; the red convertible had been towed off days ago. Bernard, if he was the one who parked it here, had known of a back entrance to the clearing. It was easy to see the tracks leading out through an open space that eventually connected with the two-track road. The men stood in the middle of the clearing and looked around. "We'd better stick together," Mitch whispered to Tom.

"Why are you whispering?" Tom whispered.

"Beats me!" Mitch whispered back. "Just seems the right thing to do. Come on. If Bernard ran into the woods when he heard us coming, maybe he left something behind. He had to be the one who opened the trunk."

They had almost made a complete circle around the clearing, fighting their way through thickets and low hanging branches, when they startled dozens of birds that were gathered around something on the ground. The birds complained loudly as they took to the sky.

"Oh, that can't be good," muttered Mitch.

"What can't be good? Since when has scaring birds become a no-no?"

"Dead things attract that kind of bird. Let's hope they were working on a deer or maybe something smaller."

"What else could it be? Bernard has killed off a big portion of the population in this town!" joked Tom. "Who's left?"

Taking the lead, Mitch arrived at the remains before Tom. "Hey buddy, you asked who's left after Bernard's one-man exterminating undertaking? Well, I'll tell you who's left. Bernard."

"Bernard? You found Bernard?"

"What's left of him."

CHAPTER 44

"ANYTHING INTERESTING?" mumbled pajama-clad Clara as she approached the breakfast table. Joe, armed with a pot of coffee and a cup in his hand, nodded.

Clara yawned, poured coffee into her favorite mug, and sat down. "I'll just pretend to be awake while you read me something interesting. Okay?"

"Oh, I won't have any trouble finding interesting stuff in today's paper, believe me! I'll stay above the fold in the paper to begin with."

"Wait a minute. You're saying there's interesting things both above and below the fold?"

"Yes, I am. Got your coffee?"

Clara nodded.

Joe cleared his throat. "'Twenty local individuals were charged in court documents unsealed today for their participation in a series of separate Medicare fraud schemes involving home health and private practice services. The Assistant Attorney General was quoted as saying, 'Today we have charged physicians, nurses, clinic owners and other medical professionals with submitting millions of dollars in false claims to Medicare.' He went on to say that the investigation had just started and more charges were pending."

"This was going on in our own little town?"

"Here's more," Joe declared. "'In a separate complaint unsealed today, five physicians and two other individuals are charged with false billing for unnecessary equipment and prescription drugs at the assisted living home recently purchased by George Wing.'"

"George Wing! That's one of the men who came into our office the day of Anita's murder. The other one tried to coax Billy back to his car."

"Ah, yes, the ever popular Bernard! Clara, remember that name, because you'll hear it again when we tackle the story below the fold in the paper."

"For heaven's sake, cut the dramatics! It's too early in the morning."

"Let's finish up this one. 'Efforts to contact Mr. Wing have not been successful. No one is answering the phone at his residence.'"

Clara wasn't sleepy anymore. "I read the other day that medical fraud was stealing billions of dollars from Medicare. You'd think someone would come up with a way to keep tabs on that program."

"They have, but the system is being used to keep track of rental movies. Ready for what's below the fold?"

"How about my making us breakfast before tackling the new story?" Clara asked. "I'm hungry."

"Better wait on breakfast. After you hear what's below the fold in today's paper, I don't think you'll be wanting anything to eat in the near future."

Clara listened, food and coffee forgotten, as Joe summarized the account of Bernard Wing, brother of George Wing, who was wanted by the police for the alleged murders of Mike Fuller, Anita Foreman, Agnes Foreman, and Harold Foreman.

Details were sketchy and the motives for the killings would always be speculative; Bernard Wing was dead, the victim of a bear mauling. Mr. Wing's body was discovered in the woods near the clearing where the car belonging to Mike Fuller, one of Bernard's alleged murder victims, had been found. Two bodies in the trunk have been identified as Agnes Foreman and her son Harold, also allegedly killed by Bernard.

Fortunately, there were no pictures of the mauled Bernard.

Clara pushed her coffee cup across the table. "Ugh. Who found Bernard?"

"Tom and Mitch. I saw Tom an hour later, and his face was still green!"

"So Bernard killed all those people and we'll never know what his motives were? Is that what the paper said?"

"That's what's in the paper. But, according to Tom, they've figured out some of them. Bernard killed Mike because Mike was going to tell George about Bernard's perverted activities and Anita just happened to be at the wrong place at the wrong time. As for Agnes, or as we knew her, Mrs. Kingham, she was hit by a car at the busy intersection going out of town. Her bag was found in a tree by a tree-trimmer. It's thought that it was pure coincidence that Bernard was driving the car that hit her. Why he killed Harold is a mystery. However, another bike was found by the clearing, so maybe Harold just accidentally stumbled on to the red convertible, and Bernard killed him."

"And to think all that was going on right here in our little town," Clara mused. "Well, George seems to have disappeared, and Bernard is dead. Should I feel bad that Bernard got mauled by a bear?"

"In my opinion, he got off easy; he was looking at serious prison time for the four murders. Anyhow, I'm still angry at him for what he tried to do to Billy."

They sat in silence. The rustling of the newspaper was the only sound in the room.

"That's it for interesting things in the paper?"

"A medical fraud uncovered and the alleged killer of four people mauled by a bear isn't enough for you?"

"I need to laugh. Anything funny in the comics?"

"Haven't read them yet. Oh, but there is something on page three. Have you been following the account of the wild animal that seems to be hauling off small dogs?"

"Really? What kind of wild animal?"

"No one has gotten close enough to know. It's mostly seen at night, and it seems it only goes for white dogs."

"Have a lot of people reported losing their white dogs?"

"Doesn't seem to be."

"So, if no one is reporting lost white dogs, whose dog is the beast stealing? The witch that keeps taking down Lucky's posters has lost a small white dog. The dog's name is S-y-n-d-e-e, pronounced Cindy."

"Must be a pedigreed pooch?"

Clara laughed. "A registered-pampered-pedigreed-pooch! Her nails are painted and she has a bow in her hair."

"How long has she been missing?"

"Longer than Lucky."

"Yesterday's paper stated that a homeowner took a shot at the beast as it crossed his yard. It was night, but he thinks he wounded it. Anyhow, he found drops of blood the next morning."

Clara yawned. "Is that it for the morning paper?"

Joe glanced at the haggard face of his wife.

"Have another bad night, love?" he asked.

"Are there any other kind?"

"I don't think either of us has slept worth a damn since Lucky…."

"Don't say it, Joe! Don't say, 'since Lucky left us'!"

"Well, he did, Clara. We have to get used to the idea that Lucky chose to leave us. Remember, he was somebody else's dog when he scratched on your office door."

"Joe, he was an abused dog! He ran away from a cruel, evil owner. Lucky had no reason to leave us."

"Clara…"

"Forget it, Joe. I don't want to talk about it anymore. The boys are still asleep so I'm going back to bed. Wake me when they get up."

Joe watched his wife burst into tears as she headed back to their bedroom. It was obvious that Clara needed sleep. With that in mind, Joe picked up the phone and silenced the ring.

CHAPTER 45

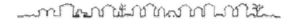

CLARA AND JOE weren't answering their phone. Had they tired of the huge dog and deserted it at the clinic? Did they think he would give him a home?

When Lucky had appeared at the clinic's door, hungry and thirsty, and full of birdshot, Dr. Phillip immediately called Clara, the owner. It was now late afternoon, and in spite of numerous calls, no one was picking up the phone.

Lucky, recovering from the minor procedure to remove the birdshot was restless. Trying to keep the big dog from walking on his wounded leg was impossible. Dr. Phillip was reminded of why they shoot horses when they break a leg. He liked the big dog that he had gotten to know after the fire truck explosion last year. The dog had thrown his body over Joe, protecting him from the blast. Lucky had almost died. Then there was the recent sleeping pill episode.

Sighing, he turned to look at the huge dog that was gazing up at him with pleading eyes.

"If only you could talk! But you can't, and I have no idea what you want me to do."

Making a guttural sound, Lucky gently gathered a bit of material from the doctors trousers and pulled.

"You want me to follow you? Is that it?"

The dog's ears went up and he struggled to his feet. He limped a few steps, and then turned around to make sure Dr. Phillip was with him. Assured that he was, Lucky led the way to the door, waited for the doctor to open it, and then, with difficulty, made his way off the porch.

When Lucky was sure he was being watched, he disappeared into a hole that had been dug under the building.

Dr. Phillip crouched down, trying to look into the hole. Listening, he could hear more than one breathing animal. What was in there with Lucky?

Remembering how thirsty Lucky had been, Dr. Phillip went back into his office and returned with a bowl of water. He placed the water by the hole, and waited.

Scuffling sounds, followed by a sharp yip didn't prepare Dr. Phillip for the sight of Lucky backing out of the hole, his teeth holding something by the scruff of its neck.

The doctor watched in amazement as Lucky turned around and gently placed a small dog at his feet. Using his nose, Lucky pushed the bowl of water toward the dog. Dragging on her stomach, she pulled herself to the bowl where she drank eagerly. The dirty bow around her neck was untied and the paint on her nails was chipped.

Lucky waited until Dr. Phillip bent down and picked her up before he turned and limped away. It was time to go home.

———————

IT HAD BEEN a quiet Sunday; the three boys had welcomed having both Joe and Clara around, paying attention to them. The loss of Lucky, Clara's crying jags, and Joe's preoccupation with the search had made living in the Skinner household unusually grim.

It was nearly dinnertime when Joe remembered that it had been hours since he had silenced the phone. He grinned, thinking how peaceful the day had been. Maybe he should do it more often? He turned the ringer back on, and he was still holding the phone when the shrill ring of an incoming call almost made him drop it. "Hello?"

"I'm suing!" screamed a voice. "You aren't getting away with this! You ruined my Syndee!"

"Wait a minute, lady! What the hell are you yelling about? You're suing me for what?"

"Oh, don't play innocent with me! Your mutt led my Syndee astray! The two of them ended up at a veterinary clinic and since my dog has an embedded chip, the vet knew to call me. I don't know how he knew Lucky, because I know for a fact that mutts don't get chips, but for some reason, the vet knew him. I want you to know that if my Syndee needs medical help after all this time, I'm not paying the bill! Not one red cent!"

"Hold on!" he yelled into the phone. "Clara, come here! Do you have any idea what this idiot is talking about?"

Clara held out her hand and took the phone. "Hello? Who is this?"

"We've met. I'm the owner of Syndee, the beautiful little dog that your Lucky ruined."

"W-what?"

"You heard me! Dr. Phillip, the vet, just called me. Your dog showed up at the clinic this morning along with Syndee."

"My dog's at the clinic?" She turned to Joe. "Lucky's found! He's at Dr. Phillip's clinic! Oh, my God, oh, my God!" She burst into tears and dropped the phone.

Joe picked it up. "I take it Dr. Phillip called you?"

"Yes, he did. I'm heading over there right now. But I meant what I said! You're going to pay for this!"

As he hung up the phone, Joe was racking his brain, trying to come up with a good defensive excuse for why he had turned off the phone's ringer.

"Grab the boys! Let's hitch the trailer to my car and head over there."

Clara and the boys were already out the door.

CHAPTER 46

TWO CARS RACED into the clinic's parking lot and screeched to a halt side by side. Car doors flew open, and the two dog owners bumped into each other.

"Get out of my way!" yelled Eileen Weber as she pushed Clara into the side of the car.

"Ha!" Clara shouted back over her shoulder as she reached the clinic's door ahead of Eileen. "I'll bet your dog can't run any faster than you!"

"At least my dog isn't ugly like yours!" panted Eileen.

"MY dog is special, and yours isn't!" taunted Clara.

"Girls, girls!" cautioned Joe. The three boys were wide-eyed watching the two women clash. "Let it go! Your dogs aren't lost any more, so cool it!"

Clara opened the door and stepped in; standing inside the waiting room sobered her. She was remembering all the hours she had spent in this room after the fire truck bomb had critically injured Lucky. The memory made her shudder.

Dr. Phillip came out of an inner room, drying his hands on a towel. "Oh, hi, Clara and Joe! I wasn't expecting to see you." Looking down at the boys' upturned faces, he smiled. "And these three gentlemen are your boys?"

"Dr. Phillip," said Joe, "meet Billy, Mackie, and Jerry."

The boys held out their hand; Dr. Phillip shook each one. "I'll bet you've been missing your big dog, haven't you?"

The boys nodded. He turned to Clara and Joe. "You two are hard to reach! I've left several messages for you today!"

Clara looked at Joe, a puzzled expression on her face.

"Later, Clara," Joe mumbled. "Later."

One look at the hateful face of the other woman sobered the doctor. "Ah, I take it you are Eileen Weber, the owner of the female dog?"

"My Syndee! I want to see my baby! What have you done with her?"

"Syndee is in the next room. You can…"

Clara interrupted. "Where's Lucky?" she demanded, trying to see around the vet. "That woman," she pointed at Eileen, "told me that Lucky and her dog showed up here. Where is he?"

"One thing at a time. Yes, the two did show up together. Lucky scratched on the door and when I opened it, there he was. He wasn't looking too good. Someone had shot him with birdshot."

"He's shot?"

"I've already taken care of that."

"Remember the article in the paper about a homeowner shooting at the beast that was dragging off small dogs?" asked Joe. "I'll bet that was Lucky and Syndee."

"So if he's all right, where is he then? I want my dog!"

"That's not the end of the story. Lucky proceeded to coax me outside. When he was sure he had my attention, he disappeared into a hole under the building. When he crawled out, he was carrying the small dog by the scruff of her neck."

"He was what?"

"Just what I said. He was carrying the small dog the way a mother dog moves her pups."

"W-w-why would he do that?" Eileen stammered. "That's crazy!"

"There's a reason why he…."

Clara interrupted. "So, where is he? I want my dog!"

Joe hugged her. "Calm down. Let the doctor talk."

Dr. Phillip shrugged. "I don't know where your dog is. After he saw that I was taking care of the little dog, he left"

"What about my dog?" demanded Eileen. "Let's talk about my dog! My Syndee is pedigreed! She has papers!"

"Your dog is in the next room; go see her."

A distressed sound came from the adjoining room. "That mutt chewed all the hair off her neck! My Syndee is ruined! Someone's going to pay for this!"

"About the miss…," Dr. Phillip turned around to explain why the hair was missing; the office was empty. Looking out the window, he saw Clara, Joe and the boys running for their car.

A sharp yelp followed by a scream came from the adjoining room. "Help! Dr. Phillip! Get in here! There's something wrong with Syndee!"

"He's got to be around here! Go slower, Joe. Boys, are you looking?" Clara was frantic.

"We've been up and down these streets three times. If Lucky was here, we'd have seen him."

"Maybe he's heading home! How many ways can he get home from here?" Clara wondered.

As he was driving up and down streets, Joe was thinking thoughts that he had no intentions of putting into words. If Lucky were wounded, might he not crawl off and hide, either to get better or to die? Dr. Phillip said he'd been shot with birdshot. Lucky wouldn't die from that, would he?

The sound of a shot jarred him.

"Turn!" Clara yelled, pointing to an upcoming intersection. "The shot came from over there!"

Running through the stop sign, Joe made the turn in time to see a man jogging, his rifle under his arm, and heading in the direction of an unmoving lump in the ditch.

"Stop the car!" she yelled to Joe.

Clara ran, knowing that if indeed it was Lucky in the ditch, his life depended on how fast she got to the man with the gun.

"No!" she screamed. "Don't shoot!"

"Stay back!" he ordered as he raised the rifle. "I just wounded it! That's the beast that's been dragging off little dogs!"

"That's no beast! That's my dog!" she cried, tackling him.

"You crazy woman!" the man yelled, trying to push Clara away. "A wounded animal is dangerous! I need to finish what I started! Get off me!"

The boys ran to the animal in the ditch. "It's Lucky!" Mackie cried. "He's dead!"

"No!" Untangling herself from the shooter, Clara ran to her dog. "He can't be dead!"

Joe grabbed the rifle out of the startled man's hand. "Mister, you'd better start praying...."

"He's not dead!" Clara shouted. "He opened his eyes! Oh Lucky, don't die on me!"

"We have to get him to Dr. Phillip!" Joe turned to the man who was retrieving his rifle from the ground where Joe had thrown it. "You have to help! I don't know how much Lucky weighs, but the three of us should be able to pick him up and put him on the trailer."

"I-I-I shot your dog?" stammered the man.

"Yes, you shot our dog. Now just don't stand there, help us pick him up!"

Joe rode with Lucky on the trailer. Clara, with tears raining down her cheeks, tried to comfort the sobbing boys in the backseat as she drove back to the clinic.

CHAPTER 47

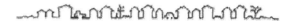

CLARA SHOOK HER head in disbelief. Once again, she was back in the clinic's waiting room praying that her dog wouldn't die. Dr. Phillip had rushed Lucky into surgery an hour ago. At some point, he was going to come through the door and look at her. What kind of look would he have on his face? Would he be smiling, telling Clara without having to say a word that her dog was still alive? Or would he stand there, his mouth not moving because he couldn't find the right words to tell her that Lucky hadn't made it?

Joe had taken the boys to Molly's house. After explaining to the family what was going on, he had asked Laurie and Kim to keep the boys busy so they wouldn't have time to think about their dog.

As Joe was saying goodbye, he noticed that the girls were already engaging his boys in an activity. It took him a few seconds to figure out just what that activity was; all five of them were sobbing.

Expecting Joe, Clara smiled when she heard someone entering the waiting room. Her smile vanished when she saw who it was.

"Oh, it's you. Run out of dogs to shoot? I hear the vet has caged ones. They should be easy marks to hit; kinda like shooting fish in a barrel."

"I'm so sorry! I can't tell you how bad I feel! My name is Steve Miller," the man said, offering his hand to Clara. She ignored it. "Really, I'm sorry! The story was in the paper! You saw it, didn't you?

About the beast that was carrying off little dogs? I thought I was doing the community a favor!"

"That beast is my big dog, Lucky. He never did anything bad in his life. And the little dog he was carrying was a white one named Syndee...." Clara's voice trailed off. "Come to think of it, Dr. Phillip never said why Lucky was carrying Syndee."

"You didn't ask? That's such an unusual thing for a dog to do, I'm just surprised you didn't."

Clara snorted. "If you knew the history of my dog, you wouldn't say something like that. By the way, why are you here?"

"Besides wanting to apologize for shooting your dog? Besides another chance to say I'm sorry? I'm here to put some meaning behind my words."

"What kind of meaning?"

"Money. I'll pick up the vet tab. I feel awful about shooting your dog."

"That's big of you. Will you pay for a box to bury him in if he doesn't make it?" Clara's voice had started out strong, but by the end, she was crying.

Joe entered the waiting room to see Clara sobbing on the shoulder of a stranger. He sat down beside her and gently pulled her to him. "Can't leave you alone for a minute!" he chuckled. "If you're gonna cry, cry on my shoulder."

"Oh, Joe!" She stopped to blow her nose. "This is Steve Miller, the man who shot Lucky."

"I recognized the trigger-happy bastard. He's got a lot of nerve, showing up here after what he did. Why is he here?"

Steve spoke up. "I came to apologize and to offer to pay the veterinary bill. It's the least I can do."

"If Lucky dies, you can pay for his burial, too," Joe muttered.

"Man, I said I was sorry!"

"Don't even talk like that, Joe! But if Lucky doesn't make it," she turned to Steve, "I'll…I'll….!"

Steve held up his hands to stop her. "I can't undo the damage I've caused. Other than paying the vet bill, there's not much else I can do."

Joe relaxed. "After what I ran into in the parking lot, it's almost a pleasure to talk to a wanna-be hero who protects the community by shooting pet dogs."

"Aw, come on, man! Lighten up!" Steve groaned.

"Who did you run into?" inquired Clara.

"That crazy Eileen Weber! She's still threatening to sue us, you know."

Steve frowned. "Sue you? For what? I'm not a lawyer, so I can't help you with that."

"So, if you're not a lawyer; what are you?"

"Besides being new in town? I'm a photographer for the local newspaper. Hey, you know that guy who got mauled by a bear? That was my first photo assignment at my new job. Man, did I get some good pictures!"

Joe looked puzzled. "There were no pictures of Bernard Wing in the paper today. The story was there, but no pictures."

Steve's mouth dropped open. "They didn't use any of them?"

"Probably too gory."

Steve hung his head. "This is not good!" He looked up at Tom. "Are you sure? Not even one?"

Joe shook his head.

"I guess I didn't impress my bosses," Steve moaned. "Not a good way to start a new job."

"There something else your bosses won't be happy about," Clara was please to tell him.

"Like what?" Steve asked.

"Well, when the readers of your paper find out who shot their favorite dog, I wouldn't want to be in your shoes!"

"Their favorite dog?"

"How long have you lived here?"

"Just this week. I was moving some of my stuff into storage when I happened to see what I thought was…well, you know what I thought."

"If you're that new in town, then you don't know about Lucky. He's made headlines at your paper several times."

"What did he do? Is he a rescue dog, or something?"

Joe laughed. "Lucky is more like 'or something'."

"Don't you dare put down my dog!" yelled Clara as she took a swipe at Joe; he ducked.

"But back to our Eileen," Joe continued. "She's all mouth…I think."

"What reason does she have for suing you?" asked Steve.

"It's her little dog Syndee that Lucky's been carrying around." He frowned. "Clara, did Dr. Phillip ever tell you why he was carrying the little dog? It's quite a trip from your office to here."

"No, he never said. I think we ran out of his office before he had a chance to say anything. Anyhow, Mr. Miller, Syndee is a pedigreed pampered pooch that Eileen says our mutt-of-a-dog ruined."

"Ruined by association?" Steve rolled his eyes.

"She's saying more than that," Joe continued. "She just told me that she doesn't want to have anything more to do with her dog since Lucky left his mongrel spit all over Syndee's neck. In her eyes, Lucky cheapened her, and she's leaving her with Dr. Phillip."

"As if Dr. Phillip needs another dog!" Clara huffed. "Joe, we know that Lucky has done some pretty wild things in the past. But can you come up with any reason he would carry a dog miles, and we are talking miles, and drop her off at a place where we took him when he was injured?"

Steve spoke up. "I don't know your dog, but I can see a connection. Is there something wrong with the little dog? Did you notice anything?"

"I've never actually seen the dog, just pictures of her. Eileen kept tacking pictures of Syndee over Lucky's posters."

"She did that?" Steve chuckled. "Wonder if her dog is as nasty as she is." He was still chuckling when the outer door opened and people rushed in. "Wow! Something big must have happened!"

"Where are you going?" Joe yelled at Steve who was pushing through the crowd, heading for the door.

"To the car to get my camera!" Steve yelled back.

Billy, Mackie, and Jerry led the way into the waiting room, followed by Laurie and Kim. Mitch and Molly were next, struggling to maneuver the twins' double stroller through the door. Tom and Marie were heard before they were seen. Logan, hanging in a sling around Tom's neck, was howling.

"Hail, hail, why is the gang all here?" a puzzled Joe bellowed the question over the baby's wail.

Clara's mouth was hanging open.

Molly stepped forward. "Clara, I apologize for starting this whole thing."

"What?"

Molly raised her voice over the baby's cry. "Clara," she yelled, "I apologize for starting this whole thing."

"What? You apologize for what? I can't hear you. Tom," she shouted over her shoulder, "can't you do something with Logan?"

"Like what?" Tom yelled back.

"I don't know! He's not my kid!"

Marie, looking haggard and weary, spoke up. "Give him to me. I'll step outside with him."

After the door closed behind Marie and Logan, the office rang with silence.

"Wow!" someone muttered.

"What were you saying?" Clara asked Molly.

"I was just explaining how we all wound up here. The kids never did quit crying, and when they found out I was coming here to support you while Lucky was in surgery, they insisted they had to come, too. And then Marie and Tom stopped at the house...." She shrugged. "It just snowballed, so here we are. Has Dr. Phillip been out to see you?"

"No," Clara said as she looked over the crowded waiting room. "Oh, here comes Steve."

The man Molly saw heading toward them was carrying a large camera. "Who's Steve?"

"He's the guy who shot Lucky."

"And you haven't killed him? He actually looks unmarked."

"I didn't lay a hand on him. He feels very bad about what he did. If Lucky doesn't make it, maybe then....." Clara covered her face with her hands. "Oh, Molly! What will I do if he doesn't make it? I can't imagine life without that dog!"

As Molly stood embracing Clara, a camera's flash startled them.

"What th...?" Molly cried.

"Sorry if I surprised you," Steve apologized.

"It's okay, Molly. Steve's a newspaper photographer."

"The man who shot your dog is taking pictures of people grieving over something that he caused? I don't think so!" Molly fumed.

Dr. Phillip stepped into the room. The doctor's eyebrows went up as he looked at the crowded waiting room. Clara was watching his mouth. Was he going to use that mouth to smile at her, or was that mouth going to form words that would crush her soul? When his eyes made contact with her red-rimmed ones, he smiled.

Clara swooned.

CHAPTER 48

JOE WAS STANDING over Clara when she finally opened her eyes.

"He smiled at me!" were the first words she said.

Dr. Phillip chuckled. "Yes, I did! I can't wait to tell my wife that a much younger woman fainted when I smiled at her."

Clara sat up. "Lucky's alive then?"

"He came through the operation fine. The bullet didn't hit anything vital; he'll be back in action in a few weeks."

"Thank you, God!" Scrambling to her feet, she mumbled, "That dog's going to be the death of me!"

Dr. Phillip looked at the familiar faces of the people who had gathered, once again, to support Clara and her dog. With the exception of the man who kept taking pictures, he knew them all. He felt honored to be involved in anything that had to do with the exceptional dog, for that's what he was.

The door opened and Marie and a sleeping Logan joined the group.

Dr. Phillip held up his hand for silence. "I know all of you would like to see Lucky. Since the small room that he's in can't handle all his admirers, I'm going to bring him out here. He's a bit groggy, so I know he would appreciate a quiet acknowledgement. No loud noises, please. Understood?"

Everyone nodded. Steve snapped a picture.

The racket of something moving on wheels became louder as it got closer. The door swung open, and Dr. Philip pushed a large flat table into the room.

On the table, with what looked like a white blanket next to his chest, lay a bandaged Lucky. Sensing her nearness, he lifted his head and searched the room for Clara. Seeing her, he struggled to get to his feet.

"No!" Dr. Phillip scolded Lucky. "Down!"

"Good boy!"

"Oh, Lucky," sobbed Clara. "I thought I'd never see you again! Can I touch him? Please?"

"Not right now, Clara."

"What if I just held his paw?"

"Later. You haven't seen it all."

"Besides Lucky? There's more?"

Sleeping Logan chose that moment to awaken; his shrill cry was piercing.

The white blanket moved. The head of a small white dog emerged, the head turning, searching for the source of the offending noise. When its eyes landed on the baby, it howled.

Logan quit crying.

Clara exclaimed, "That's not a blanket! That's Syndee. I'd know her anywhere!"

Dr. Phillip nodded. "Yes, that's Syndee."

"If that's Syndee, then where's Eileen? Why isn't she here?"

The baby took a big breath and picked up where he'd left off.

The little dog howled.

Logan quit crying.

"Ah, I think Eileen has a problem. She claims that her dog has been ruined by associating with Lucky."

Clara snorted. "My dog is special. Just because her dog...." Joe's nudge silenced her.

Logan stirred, squirmed, and opened his mouth; Syndee yipped. The baby closed his eyes.

An excited Joe turned to Tom. "Hey, buddy," he whispered, "have you noticed what Syndee's doing?"

Tom nodded, and replied softly. "She's doing something that neither Marie nor I can do. We can't keep him quiet. Our landlord is threatening to kick us out because all the neighbors are complaining about Logan's big voice."

"Did you hear what Dr. Phillip said? The owner of Syndee doesn't want her back. She claims Lucky cheapened her somehow."

"Really? Doesn't anyone else want her?"

"I don't think so. The owner said Dr. Phillip could keep her, but I doubt if the vet wants another dog."

"I-I-I don't know." Tom stepped close to Joe and whispered. "I wonder what Marie would say about adding a dog to our family?"

Joe whispered back. "If it means you won't have to move, she'd be crazy to say no."

Dr. Phillip cleared his throat. When all the conversation stopped, he carefully picked up the little white dog and held her high.

"Syndee was hit by something, probably a car." The vet slowly turned her around, showing two splinted legs. "Since both her back legs were broken, she couldn't walk."

Clara gasped. "Lucky brought her to you!"

"Yes, Lucky carried her many miles to bring her to me."

After a moment of stunned silence, the vet added, "They weren't in bad shape when they got here; he must have been finding food for both of them somewhere."

Clara rubbed her eyes; she was seeing spots. Steve had a trigger-finger when it came to both guns and cameras. It was hard to think with all those flashes going off, but she did remember the empty dog food bag she had found in the wooded patch.

The volume of noise rose in the room; chatter, laughter, rolled eyes, and shrugs greeted the news of Lucky's newest venture. Logan stirred. Marie's frantically waving hand, begging them to be quiet, was ignored. When the baby opened his mouth and wailed, all it took from Syndee was a little yip. Logan changed his mind and went back to sleep.

Marie studied her husband, wondering how hard it would be to talk him into taking the dog home with them. Maybe, with Syndee's help, they wouldn't have to move.

Wiping her eyes and swallowing a big lump in her throat, Clara gazed lovingly at her dog. Her Lucky wasn't lost. She thought back on all those days that she had filled with fears and tears, believing that her dog was gone forever. Now she knew that Lucky hadn't left her because he wanted to live with someone else; he'd deserted her to save that horrible pampered pedigreed pooch. Well, she had to admit, the dog wasn't the one that was horrible. In fact, Syndee was rather cute; it was Eileen who was horrible.

Yet, it was upsetting to think that her dog was nothing more than a typical male; they all were swayed by fancy bows and painted nails.

CHAPTER 49

STEVE MILLER WAS enjoying the first week on his new job. Not only were his pictures plastered all over the front-page of the morning paper, an article under his byline described the latest Lucky-eye-rolling escapade. Allen Real Estate was enjoying it, too. The phones were ringing; Clara was once again reaping the benefits that had followed each of Lucky's previous impressive performances.

Until Molly found live-in help, Clara was the only realtor in the office. It reminded her of the time when Molly was pregnant and had to stay home, off her feet. Was she going to have to call in the mothers again? Mitch's mother, Marilyn, had allowed her real estate license to lapse, but she could still produce a smashing comparative market analysis. Molly's mother, Peggy, who had never worked outside the home, found that she loved answering phones in the busy office.

Clara was swamped. The calls poured in from sellers who wanted her to list their houses and from buyers who wanted her to sell them a house. No matter how overwhelmed she became, she took time for an occasional glance at the sleeping dog. He was safe, but the past days when she hadn't known if her dog was dead or alive had left her with deep wounds.

She and Joe had agreed that in the afternoon when Lucky walked to the station to be with Joe, Clara would walk with him. When it was time for him to go back to Clara at the end of the day, Joe would walk him there. The hitch and the trailer would be permanent fixtures on Clara's car.

"So, we're back to walking Lucky? I thought we had solved the walking problem when Dave came up with the trailer."

"Just give me time, Joe. I'm sure I'll get over this…this not trusting him."

Joe snorted. "You think the two of you should go to a marriage counselor?"

Clara blushed. "Those days when Lucky was gone," she shook her head, "Who would've thought that I could love such an ugly mutt so deeply?"

"Is Syndee still at the clinic?"

"Yes, and she'll be there for the next couple of weeks before she's released."

"Do you have any idea how Tom talked Marie into giving Syndee a home?"

"Turns out, after they saw what Syndee could do with Logan, they both wanted the dog. However, Tom thought he was going to have to sweet-talk Marie into taking the dog, and Marie thought she was going to have trouble talking Tom into the same thing. I heard the conversation; it would have made a good routine for Abbot and Costello."

"Wish I'd heard it," chuckled Joe.

"You know, Joe, life is pretty good. Bernard, the boogey man who gave me nightmares, is dead. We have Lucky, albeit a little lame, and Tom and Marie won't have to move, thanks to Syndee. How's that for a happy ending?"

"In case no one has ever said all's well that ends well, I'm gonna say it."

"Nice try, Joe!" laughed Clara.

CHAPTER 50

"WHAT DO YOU MEAN…he didn't get there?"

"Exactly what I said. He didn't get here."

"Am I going to have to start worrying again? It's been four months since he put me through that Syndee fiasco."

"I haven't forgotten. You have to admit, Lucky hasn't given us anything to worry about since. He's been a model dog, our Lucky!"

"Joe, you're forgetting that one day he didn't show up for forty-five minutes. We never did figure out where he went."

"Yes, and I remember the hours you spent trying to get him to tell you. I should have filmed it. By now, it would have had a million hits on YouTube."

"Oh, for heaven's sake, quit joking around. He should have been there thirty minutes ago. Go back outside and look for him."

Clara chewed on the end of her pen until Joe picked up the phone.

"He's not here, Clara."

"Here we go again," she sighed. "I just have to remember that he's done this before, and he did come back."

Deep in thought, Clara sat with the phone in her hand. It was true. Lucky, with the exception of that one day right after the Syndee debacle, had stuck to the routine. Why did he break it today? What was he up to now?

Sighing, she hung up the phone and surveyed the busy office. Marilyn Hatch was at the computer, her fingers flying over the keys, pounding out one comparative market analysis after another. Peggy

222

Allen was in her glory. If there ever was a Phone Queen, it was Peggy. Molly was still at home, taking care of the twins and the girls. Their latest attempt at getting live-in help was centered on a Swedish au pair. They had worked with an international agency that had put them in touch with Agda, a lovely-sounding young lady. After many over-seas phone conversations, she was on her way to Michigan. If Agda worked out, Molly would return to work.

Marilyn shut down the computer, took her coffee cup to the sink, picked up her purse, and turned to Clara. "It's time to go home, Clara. How long are you going to sit here and wait for Lucky?"

Clara just shook her head. "I knew he was up to something! When he broke the routine this morning, I had a bad feeling. He's doing it again."

"Doing what?"

Clara shrugged. "Whatever it is that Lucky wants to do, I guess. I'm waiting for Joe. He's coming to the office to stay with me."

Knowing that there were no words in the English language that would ease Clara's pain, Marilyn just hugged her.

The office was silent except for an occasional escaped sigh from Joe or a swallowed sob from Clara. It was way past closing time.

"We can't stay here all night, Clara. We have three boys at home with the sitter. It isn't fair to them."

"I know. Know what I was thinking about?"

"Not fair," Joe teased.

"Okay, I'll admit it. Lucky can't talk and you can't read my mind, so I'll just tell you. I was remembering the day I was sitting right here at this desk when something scratched at the door. I opened it up, and a huge blood-covered animal fell in."

"Have you ever thought how your life would be different now if you had called someone to come and remove the dog? That was an option you had, you know. You didn't have to keep him."

Clara chuckled. "I can hear the conversation now. 'Could you please send someone over with a crane to remove a huge beast from my doorway?'"

"Considering that no one in town owns a crane, your wait would have been a long one! But you had a choice! You could have gotten rid of him, you know. If you had, just think how different our lives would be right now. You would never have walked past the fire station, and we would never have met," mused Joe. "That would have been a tragedy. I don't even want to imagine my life without you."

"The fickle finger of fate," nodded Clara. "And I would still be in competition with the Goodyear blimp." She shivered, remembering. "Okay, go unplug the coffee and I'll start locking up."

As Clara stood by the door preparing to close up the office, it flew open and the entire Hatch brood noisily swept past her into the room.

With a surprised look on her face, Molly asked, "What are the two of you doing here? It's way past closing time!"

"Well, I could ask the same thing about you," Clara retorted.

"We went out to eat at the new restaurant on Pine. I recommend it. Good food!"

"I didn't ask for a culinary opinion on the new restaurant," Clara reminder her, "I asked why are you showing up at the office so late in the day?"

"I just dropped in to pick up some files for the end of the month report. Lady, if you keep on selling the way you have been since the Syndee episode, I'll be able to hire an accountant!"

"I don't take any credit for the increased business. That was all Lucky's doings."

"That dog! By the way, where is he? He's usually asleep in the corner over there, but I see that his bed is empty."

"That's because he never showed up this afternoon when he was supposed to go to Joe at the station,"

"Not again!"

"Yes, again. That dog is making an old woman out of me," wailed Clara. "All I can say, he'd better have a good story!"

The first scratch was tentative. The second scratch was louder.

"Honey, did you hear that?"

"Hear what?"

"Go open the door. I think I heard something."

Laurie and Kim hid behind Molly.

Another scratch sent Clara flying across the room. Since it was almost dusk, and since thing have a way of looking different in the half-light, what she saw when she opened the door made her gasp.

"J-J-Joe, would you please come here?"

"What's wrong?"

"Please tell me you see what I see."

"Something the matter with your eyes?" he ribbed her. "I'll tell you what I…oh, my God!"

Curious to see what had caused such a shocking response, the Hatches stumbled over the double stroller to crowd around Joe and Clara.

Two huge dogs stared back at them. One of them was Lucky. The other one, a female with low-hanging teats, was almost as big as Lucky. Each dogs was carrying a pup by the scruff of its neck.

Stunned by the unexpected sight, no one made a sound. The lengthy silence was broken by Laurie.

"Puppies," she yelled.

"Puppies!" Kim repeated. "Lucky's puppies!"

Turning to Mitch and Molly, Laurie cried, "Both of you said we could have a dog if it was another Lucky!"

"You promised!" squealed Kim. "We get a puppy, we get a puppy, we...."

"That's quite enough," muttered Mitch.

Molly groaned.

Laying his pup down at Clara's feet, Lucky looked up at her with begging eyes.

"Oh, my God," cried Clara. "Lucky's a dad! He wants to show me his baby!" Stooping down, she picked up the ball of fur. "Such a cute little baby, yes you are, you cute little rascal," she crooned. "Who's the cutest puppy? You are, yes, you are, you...."

"Clara!" Joe spoke sharply.

Clara had the grace to blush. "Ah, how old do you think these pups are?"

"Their eyes are open, so they're at least three weeks old," Joe guessed.

No one was paying any attention to the mother's growing agitation as Clara laid her cheek on the warm pup in her hands. A low growl startled them all.

"Whoa!" whispered Joe. "Everyone back off. We don't know anything about the female."

Lucky moved close to the bitch and grunted; the dogs touched noses. The female dog whined, placed her pup on the ground, and backed up.

Kim picked up the pup and clutched it to her chest. She whispered to Laurie, "Do you really think they'll let us keep it?"

"How could they not? That's another Lucky if I ever saw one," Laurie whispered back.

Molly anxiously eyed the mother dog who was watching Kim holding her pup. "Do you think the mother dog's a problem?"

"Looks like Lucky has everything under control," chuckled Joe. "Why am I not surprised?"

Clara cuddled the pup in her hands. "I'll bet this is what Lucky looked like when he was a puppy. Aren't you just a little cutie? Yes, you are, you are a precious pup…."

"Whoa!" cautioned Joe. "Let's not get too attached here, woman! Does the female have a collar?"

Not wanting to get too close to the dog, all eyes searched her neck.

"Anyone see a collar?" asked Joe. "I sure don't."

"Well, if she has an owner, we know that it's someone within walking distances," Mitch reasoned.

Clara shrugged. "Since I'm the poster queen of this crowd. I'll make up some tomorrow and plaster the neighborhood with them. But what if she's a stray? What if no one shows up to claim her?" She turned to Joe. "Could we keep her?"

Joe raised his eyebrows. "Two huge dogs, two puppies, and three boys in our little house? Would there be room for the two of us?"

"Aw, come on, Joe. It wouldn't be that bad!"

The crowd grew silent.

"Well, whatever we decide, we'll have to keep her at least for several more weeks," Joe reasoned. "These pups are a long way from being weaned."

"Then, after that, what? What if no one claims her?"

He looked over at Clara who was still snuggling one of the pups. "We do have options."

"We do?"

"Yes, we do. It's just as it was when Lucky first scratched on your door. You could have called someone to come and cart him off."

"I'm so glad I didn't do that!" Clara whispered, hugging the pup. "So tell me again, what are our choices?"

Joe cleared his throat. "After the pups are weaned, Laurie and Kim get one…" he had to pause while Mitch attempted to get the screaming girls under control…"and we keep the other pup. Then, if no one has claimed the female, we can hire someone to come and remove her from our premises, or…"

Clara cringed. "Oh, Joe, there has to be a better option than that!"

"You didn't let me finish!"

"Okay, I'll play your silly game. Or what?"

Laughing, Joe grabbed her and swung her around. "Or, we can buy a bigger house and keep her. Which will it be?"

The top realtor in town just grinned.

About the Author

EVELYN LIVES WITH HER husband, Barry, in a home they built on the shores of lovely Pearl Lake near Traverse City, Michigan. She loves pets and currently shares her home with Earl, a dog from the Humane Society, and Simon, a cat that coyotes were eyeing for lunch.

The daughter of a coal miner, Evelyn left the hills of Pennsylvania to attend Anderson College in Indiana and then to Michigan where she earned a Masters at Wayne State University.

She taught school until the birth of her two children, Jill and Tom. A constant delight in her life is her stepdaughter, Judith. Before retirement, Evelyn spent the last fifteen years of her working life as a Realtor in Rochester, Michigan.

A life-long issue with Restless Legs Syndrome instigated the start of her writing career. Her first book, And So To Sleep, was begun on a sleepless night. The themes of restless legs and real estate run through the entire series.

Evelyn would love to hear from you. Contact her at evharp@hotmail.com, or find out much more about her on her website at www.evelynallenharper.com.

CPSIA information can be obtained at www.ICGtesting.com
Printed in the USA
BVOW071246190312

285517BV00001B/7/P